THE STEAM CHASERS:

THE BOUNDLESS

BLACKPRINT

By: Dr. Doresa A. Jennings

Dr. Doresa A. Jennings

Book #3

The Boundless Blackprint

For all the kids that have wondered to themselves where they fit in their neighborhoods, communities, cities, states, countries, and even the world. The answer is that you fit everywhere.

Sincerely,

Dr. Doresa A. Jennings

This book is a work of fiction. Any references to historical events, real people, or real locations are used fictitiously. Other names, characters, places, and incidents are the product of the author's imagination, and any resemblance to actual events or locals or persons is entirely coincidental.

Doresa Ayanna Publications
DoresaAyanna.com
©2020

ISBN: 978-1-951054-08-3

Library of Congress Control Number: 2020951101

Table of Contents

 Chapter 1

"Come on, ring!" Terrence didn't know if he was just thinking the words or if they actually came out of his mouth. It seemed like ages since his big brother, Trevor, said he would call him with the news. It was times like these that Terrence realized just how much he missed his brother, who was away at college. People were sometimes surprised by how close their friendship was, even though his brother was seven years older than he was. Terrence's big brother was a part of almost every great memory he had growing up. He'd taught Terrence how to ride a bike and a skateboard, let him help when he changed the oil in his car, and even helped him build his first airplane model. Terrence still had the model up on a bookshelf in his bedroom. His brother helped him put it together so that Terrence would feel better about his dad being away at work. Terrence's dad worked for the Army Corps of Engineers and often had to be away on projects for weeks at a time. His brother would step in whenever he could to lend a hand.

When it was time for his brother to leave for college, Terrence had cried almost as much as his mother. Like the great big brother he had always been, Trevor had kept his promise and called Terrence at least once a week since he had left for college in August. Their calls were usually short, telling each other about their crazy experiences. But this call was going to be different. This call was huge. This call was important. Just when Terrence thought the wait would kill him, the phone rang.

He ran for the phone, forgetting Diego was sitting next to him. Diego barked as a sign of indignation as Terrence almost landed on him as he reached for the phone.

"Hello!" Terrence almost yelled into his phone, trying to make his voice carry over his now angry dog.

"What in the world is going on? Why is Diego making all that noise?" Trevor seemed to be talking just as loud as Terrence.

"Oh, he's fine. He was on my bed and the phone scared him." Terrence tried to sound convincing.

"Diego isn't scared of a phone. Now, what Diego might be scared of is someone jumping across the bed and probably crushing him in the process!" Trevor was now laughing as he spoke.

"How did you know that?" asked Terrence.

"I'm your big brother, I know everything. Anyway, I just got word this morning."

Terrence could hardly contain himself. "And what did they say?"

"Calm down, I'm trying to tell you. You can let your friends know I will be your official VIP tour guide when you all come to Washington, DC. I even made arrangements for you all to get a behind-the-scenes tour of the campus. That should impress the ladies all right, showing that you already have a college hook-up. Maybe impress Shar the most." Trevor was now laughing hysterically.

"Dude, don't say things like that. I don't even like her. Besides, we're all coming to learn about American history. Is your college a part of American history?" Terrence was looking in the mirror hanging on his door, trying to see if he was turning red. His face always felt hot when his brother teased him about liking someone.

"What kind of question is that? We're talking about Howard University. Founded in 1867, one of the most prestigious universities in the world. Don't you think a place that is over one hundred and fifty years old is a part of American history? You need this tour really bad. But I'll take care of you, little bro, no worries. Now, I have to run; tell Shar I said hi." Still laughing, Trevor hung up the phone.

Terrence could ignore his brother's teasing because he was so excited about what Trevor had said. They were going to get a VIP tour, courtesy of his brother. This was going to be epic! Terrence put his phone in his pocket, grabbed his backpack, and headed toward the kitchen. He had spent so much time waiting for his brother to call, he hadn't had time to sit down and eat breakfast.

"So nice of you to join me for breakfast, thankfully I get thirty seconds of attention before you have to run out the door." Terrence's mother was standing in the kitchen, holding out her hand.

"Yes! You thought about me." Terrence reached for the egg sandwich his mother had made while he had been upstairs.

"So, what's the word?" asked Mrs. Faulkner.

"Trevor is giving us a tour! We even get to go see his college." As the words came out of his mouth, he felt even more excited.

"Well, get going, you don't want to be late. I'm sure your friends will be excited to hear the news. Washington, DC better watch out, the STEAM Chasers are coming to town." With those words, she gave Terrence a kiss on the cheek as he stepped out the door.

Terrence got to school faster than he ever had before. He knew he had left a little later than normal since he'd waited for his brother's call, and he wanted to make sure he had time to tell the other STEAM Chasers the good news before class started.

***

Terrence finally made it to the classroom after making a quick stop at his locker. He didn't need anything, he just wanted to give himself time to stop breathing so hard from running all the way to school before he went to meet up with his friends. When he walked into the room, he saw Ebony, Shar, Marcus, Akiya, and Chase gathered at one of the circular tables they often used for group projects. Ebony was holding a postcard in her hand. As Terrence approached, he heard her talking.

"I got this package in the mail yesterday. I was nervous when I saw it was from Space Camp, like maybe they wanted their medal back or something. So I thought I would wait to open it here with you guys, you know, in case I needed some moral support." Ebony looked around at her friends.

"They definitely aren't asking for their medal back, they're probably writing to tell you they want to hire you or you got chosen to be an astronaut or something like that." Marcus was now moving closer to her with a keen eye on the letter.

Shar spoke up next. "I'm with Marcus, which surprises me. They would definitely try to give you a job before they asked for that Right Stuff Award back. No one takes back that kind of award."

Chase stepped in a bit closer. "Yeah, the only way they would want that award back is if they found out you were a part of the plan to steal the rocket. But I'd never tell, no matter how much they tortured me. Your part of the great rocket heist is safe with me, Ebony!"

Akiya looked like she was going to burst. "Chase, we were just kidding! No one was going to actually try to steal the rocket for real. Don't be silly."

Chase and Marcus looked at each other in a way that Terrence knew all too well. Since he'd been their roommate at Space Camp, he knew their dreams of flying off into the universe were more real than the girls probably recognized. Thankfully, Space Camp was fun enough without the need to be shot into space for real, and the team did so well, they'd been invited to come back and attend Aviation Challenge on a research scholarship. Terrence smiled to himself; The STEAM Chasers had struck again and inspired even more people. That really made him proud to be a part of the team.

Shar put her hand on Ebony's shoulder. "Well, you might as well open the package. I am dying to know what's in it!"

Ebony looked at Akiya, who gave her a thumbs up. She slowly opened the envelope. So slowly, in fact, that it looked like Marcus just might fall out from anticipation.

She pulled out a postcard. "Hey, it's from Tai!"

The postcard had a picture of the Saturn V Rocket. Terrence felt a surge of energy flow through him. He really did have a great time at Space Camp, and he thought building the rockets just may have been his favorite part.

Ebony turned the postcard over and began reading. *"Dear Ebony, I hope this package finds you well. Someone wanted to write you a letter, and because we couldn't give out your address, I let them send it to me at Space Camp and told them that I would send it along. The patches your team made are also complete now, your design was incredible. Let Shar, Terrence, Akiya, Marcus, and Chase know we said hello from Space Camp and can't wait to see you all again."*

"Wait, they made the patches we designed into real patches? Like the mission patches astronauts get each time they fly?" Now Marcus really looked like he might faint.

Ebony pulled out the patches and passed one to each member of the group.

"Hey, all the words are spelled right!" The words came out of Terrence's mouth before he even had time to think. Having something spelled wrong that was going to be sort of permanent was always a fear of his, particularly because he had dyslexia. He caught Ebony's eye, and she was flashing a huge smile. She was also dyslexic, and a spelling mistake had been discovered in front of the entire camp, but they had gotten through it together.

"A mission patch must mean they expect us to get ahold of that rocket and launch it after all. I love Space Camp!" Chase was trying to use tape to stick the patch on to his shirt.

"I don't think that is what they mean, Chase. And that tape isn't going to work either. If you want, I can sew it onto your shirt. I might sew mine on my favorite jacket." Terrence was reaching out his hand to get Chase's patch.

"You sew?" asked Shar.

Terrence felt his face go flush. "Yeah, a little. Sometimes when I'm working on models of planes or cars, I like to customize the elements a bit. Being able to sew lets me make my own parachutes and things like that. It isn't hard. I can teach you."

"Sewing party at Terrence's house!" Marcus could turn anything into a party. But it actually seemed like a fun idea.

"That would be so cool! We can learn to sew on our patches and reminisce about Space Camp. Now, what was the letter Tai mentioned?" Akiya was looking back to the package Ebony had placed on the table.

"Oh yeah, I got so caught up in the patches, I forget about that part." Ebony pulled out the letter. "Wow!"

"What?" Akiya's eyes got big as she looked at Ebony with concern.

"It's from Garth." Ebony looked at the letter as if it might spring to life and bite her.

"Now I'm very curious. Go ahead and read it, Ebony, we've got your back." Chase was looking serious as he spoke.

Ebony opened this letter much more quickly than the package, and she started reading quickly. "*Dear Ebony, I was writing to say that I am sorry for how I treated you at Space Camp. It wasn't fair to take my*

11

jealousy out on you. I want you to know that I think you are a great scientist, and I am sorry I tried to embarrass you. It wasn't right, and it wasn't fair. I hope you will forgive me. I also hope to see you at the science fair again next year. I am working on a project that has nothing to do with space, but it is something that I really like. It is going to be hydraulic pumps, that's more my speed. Also, can you tell Terrence that I think it was really cool that he remembered my name? I don't know how his memory is so good. Maybe he can eventually remember me for something good and not when I wasn't on my best behavior. Anyway, let all the STEAM Chasers know that I'm sorry, and if we have a chance to meet again, it will be good next time. Sincerely, Garth."

Marcus was the first to break the silence. "Whoa, we are pretty awesome. We basically helped Kylo Ren turn back into Ben Solo!"

Chase jumped in. "If we were at Hogwarts, we could have totally turned Voldemort back into Tom Riddle."

Terrence thought for a second and said, "Wasn't Tom Riddle kind of evil in the first place?"

Akiya gave Terrence a smile. "Focus, everyone; let's just relish the fact that Garth isn't going to be a bully anymore. I bet he is really a good person."

"He was willing to write an apology letter when he didn't have to; that definitely says something." Ebony was putting the letter back into the envelope now.

Shar turned to Terrence. "You ran in pretty quickly. Did you have something to tell us?

"Yes!" Terrence realized he had spoken much louder than he had anticipated. He took a breath and spoke a bit softer. "I talked to my brother this morning. He volunteers with an organization that takes people on African American focused tours of Washington, DC. He has permission to take us on our very own VIP tour! We get backstage passes to the coolest parts of the National Museum of African American History and Culture, and he is even going to take us on a tour of his school."

"VIP? So we are very important people in Washington, DC, and we haven't even gotten there yet? Yes, this is exactly how my life should be!" Marcus put his hands behind his head and looked around the room as if he was a superstar.

"What school does your brother go to again?" asked Akiya.

"Howard University," responded Terrence.

"Our first college tour; this is going to be amazing!" Shar looked like she was going to explode.

"Yeah, and they will realize how smart Akiya is and just tell her she can skip high school and go straight there!" Chase laughed as Akiya shot him a look.

"Ha, ha, Chase. However, from what I remember, your grades aren't too shabby either."

"Well, no way am I skipping high school. Marcus and I have already started planning out some of our high school adventures. We won't consider ourselves ready for college until the puppy army has become a reality."

"The puppy army. Not the 'Am I Being Detained Device,' but the puppy army. That's your priority?" Shar looked at Marcus disapprovingly.

"No, my priority is the app that I am working on for you, right after I put the finishing touches on Ebony's. She even took hers for a test run, and it works. Ebony will soon always know the optimal nights for stargazing, thank you very much."

Shar shook her but still smiled. "Sorry, Chase, I shouldn't have judged you."

"Well, if you really meant it, you should have spoken those words in Python."

"I can't speak Python." Shar seemed like she was ready to pull back her apology.

"No, you can't speak Python, despite the fact that I've tried to teach it to you for years. But you should at least learn to say sorry in it."

Akiya stepped closer to Chase. She loved all languages and wanted to learn to greet people in as many languages as possible. "How exactly would someone say sorry in Python?"

"All this talk about Python, I'm starting to wonder if Chase might be Tom Riddle." Marcus laughed, seemingly to break the tension.

"That's parseltongue," said Terrence.

"Snake language is snake language." Marcus shrugged his shoulders.

"You, Shar, made a ValueError, which happens when a function gets an argument of correct type but improper value. You knew I was capable of creating a puppy army but incorrectly determined the army was more important than other things. You incorrectly guessed how I valued it. So apologize."

Shar gritted her teeth then smiled overly sweetly and said, "Sorry for the ValueError, Chase."

"All is forgiven, since you spoke in Python code and all!" Chase and Shar then burst out laughing and didn't stop until Mrs. Worthington stepped inside the classroom and asked everyone to find a comfortable spot to sit in so they could begin their schoolwork for the day.

 Chapter 2

"Okay class, let's get started." Mrs. Worthington bounded into the room with a big smile on her face. "Everyone, have a seat while we discuss some details for our upcoming trip to Washington, DC."

Shar, Ebony, and Akiya sat down on the comfortable tan couch located just in front of the reading area. The three seemed to have a magical ability to always get the most coveted seating area in the entire classroom. Chase pulled up a bean bag chair near the couch, and Terrence was surprised that Ebony didn't have a reaction when Chase dropped the chair so close to her it almost landed on her foot. Marcus grabbed a folding chair from the back wall, unfolded it next to where Chase had placed his bean bag chair, and sat down.

"Thank you again for the folding chair, **Mr. Nathanial Alexander**!" Marcus spoke loudly enough for the entire class to hear.

"You're welcome, my son, have fun sitting."

The entire class burst out laughing as Chase tried to keep a straight face. He had been practicing ventriloquism and had gotten pretty good at making funny statements without his mouth moving even an inch. But he usually broke character quickly enough that even if his voice wasn't discernable, the look on his face was. It took less than three seconds before Chase was laughing so hard, he rolled off the chair and onto the floor.

"That is exactly what you get for trying to take credit for the work of a master. And how dare you call me son—I'm older than you by an entire week! So, I'm sonning you—son!" Marcus gave Chase a friendly push.

"Alright, you two, settle down," Mrs. Worthington spoke from the front of the room.

Terrence sat down on the floor on the other side of the couch. He was closest to Shar and so he heard her speaking.

"How does she do that?" asked Shar, almost to no one.

"Do what?" asked Akiya.

Terrence was glad Akiya asked the question because he had no idea what Shar was talking about either, but he didn't know if it would be rude to ask. He was pretty sure she wasn't talking to him, and he didn't want her to know he might be eavesdropping. Then he wondered if it really was eavesdropping if you weren't listening on purpose, the other person was just speaking loudly enough for you to hear what they were saying. He didn't get too deep into that thought because Shar was answering Akiya now, and that sort of answered his question since he left his own thoughts to listen.

"Her hair. Mrs. Worthington always has perfect hair. And it changes all the time! She must have a master beautician."

Terrence looked at Mrs. Worthington. He hadn't really noticed before but thought Shar just might be correct. Today, Mrs. Worthington's hair was braided in what looked like patterns. Each braid was going in its own direction before it eventually led around the side of her head and down her back.

"That's cool, what are those things called, Shar?" Chase also must have been eavesdropping, and Terrence was once again glad that someone else asked the question he had in his mind.

"What makes you think I know?" Shar tried to sound serious, but Terrence could see her crack a smile.

"Because you are the queen of all things fashion, and you personally wrote a letter to my dad saying that while the scavenger hunt was great, he neglected to add **Lyda D. Newman** to the list, who received a patent for a hairbrush in 1898. So, you know what that hairstyle is called, you might as well spill it!" Marcus sat back and folded his arms, clearly feeling triumphant.

"Fine. They're called cornrows, and Mrs. Worthington's look amazing." Shar seemed to be taking in the style as if she were filing it away in a mental database.

"My mom used to cornrow my hair all the time when I was younger, but it never looked like that. Of course, it looks a heck of lot better than when my dad tried to cornrow my hair. That was a disaster!" Ebony was shaking her head.

Akiya was now laughing out loud. "Sorry to laugh, but I totally remember that, Ebony. You even came to school like that."

"I know! I told my dad he was never allowed to cornrow my hair again. I don't think I've worn my hair like that since. But if it could look like Mrs. Worthington's, I just might."

"Thanks for the compliment, ladies, but let's get back to our class topic." Mrs. Worthington gave the group a gentle look.

"Well, we have information to share. Shar can tell you all about hairstyles and **Lyda Newman's** hairbrush." Marcus gave a dramatic wave in Shar's direction.

Shar looked at Marcus and started to say something. Akiya must have known it was going to be bad, so she quickly interrupted.

"I have a history question that has to do with cornrows, Mrs. Worthington. I read that during times of slavery, African American women would get their hair cornrowed into patterns that could be used as maps for the Underground Railroad, is that true?"

"That is a great question, Akiya!" Mrs. Worthington beamed at Akiya.

"We know that women of African descent have been braiding their hair in elaborate styles since at least 3000 BCE. There were depictions of women with cornrows in Stone Age paintings in the Tassili Plateau of the Sahara. And you are correct. There have been numerous accounts of African American women having maps created through the patterns of cornrows to help guide enslaved people to freedom. Unfortunately, due to the secretive nature of the

Underground Railroad, we don't have reliable written records of this happening. However, the stories are so numerous that many historians have come to the conclusion that there is at least some truth to this assertion."

"Oh my gosh, that is awesome. Now I really want to give cornrows another chance!" The words flew out of Ebony's mouth so fast she almost surprised herself.

"Well, I'm only getting them if I can go to Mrs. Worthington's stylist," said Shar.

"Or maybe Mr. Parvin will hook us all up." Chase was patting his head and laughing, probably because his hair was clearly too short to cornrow.

"Speak for yourself, I already look good!" Marcus smoothed back his locs. "Maybe I will give you all the history of locs for our next 'how is he so handsome' discussion."

Now it was Akiya who almost hit the floor laughing. Terrence knew it wasn't in jest though, everyone talked about how good Marcus' locs looked.

And he'd noticed more and more kids with starter locs after Marcus got his.

"Well, we absolutely look forward to your history lesson. However, it will have to wait for another time; now we need to talk about our trip." With that, the class gave Mrs. Worthington their attention.

Terrence's mind immediately went back to the conversation with his brother. A VIP tour of Washington, DC was great, but mainly, he was excited about getting to spend time with Trevor again, although he wondered what his friends would think. Terrence was always the person who kept Chase and Marcus out of trouble, would they be ready for the Terrence who could hold his own in joke contests with a college student?

"What is that goofy smile about?"

Terrence jumped. How long had Shar been looking at him? How long had he been smiling?

"He was probably thinking about our VIP tour!" Chase and Marcus were going over a crazy handshake they had been trying to perfect for the last two weeks.

Marcus chimed in, "You mean my VIP tour. I'm sure Terrence's brother has heard about my fame and just invited the rest of you along so you wouldn't feel bad."

Ebony started shaking her head. "If this trip is anything like Space Camp, you might need to be focusing on packing rather than what happens after we get there, Marcus."

Marcus cracked a smile. "Touché, Ebony. I guess I need to start getting my college student wardrobe ready, or maybe I should focus on looking like a politician, even a president. Hey, Chase, you got a tan suit I can borrow?"

"Why would I have a tan suit? And why would I let you borrow it if I had a tan suit? I mean—I'm presidential, maybe I'll wear the tan suit."

Akiya sighed loudly. "I guess since I'm clearly the only person actually paying attention to what Mrs. Worthington is saying, I'll share my notes with you all."

"Or we could stop being rude and pay attention. Sorry!" Terrence grabbed his pen and started writing. He reminded himself to hit the record button on his pen while he wrote. It was one of his dyslexia accommodations and would record what was being said at the same time as he was taking notes. That way, if he missed anything the teacher said or couldn't read one of the words he misspelled, he could go back and listen to the recording. After a few minutes, he looked at his paper and felt a sense of pride; not only could he read all of his handwriting, he was also pretty sure he'd spelled the word 'expeditiously' correctly.

 Chapter 3

Terrence was surprised at how fast the first part of the school day went with everyone talking about the trip to DC. He walked into the cafeteria and saw Chase and Marcus already sitting down. As he approached, the cousins looked up in unison and greeted him with a big smile.

"Oh no, I know that look. This isn't going to be good, is it?" Terrence placed his lunch on the table as he sat down.

"No, Terrence, this isn't good. This is great! One of our best ideas ever." Chase was bobbing up and down as if he was a tea kettle about to explode.

"If this has anything to do with puppy armies or stealing rockets, I'm going to have to pass." Terrence was thinking about all the ways Marcus and Chase had pushed the envelope. "I thought for sure you two would be on some government watchlist by now."

"No, it isn't anything big like that, although we may need to start thinking about options, we are going to the nation's capital after all! There has to be something worth doing big!" Marcus raised his eyebrows at Terrence as if he was already considering ways to make himself famous on the upcoming class trip.

"In the meantime, we're just trying to figure out a good way to prank the girls." Chase bumped Marcus who turned and gave him a high five.

"So, instead of getting on a government watch list, you decided to go straight to dead? Okay, that sounds fun. Good luck with that!" Terrence started to pack his lunch back up.

"No way, man. You're a part of this too. Besides, it will help us pass the time. We aren't going to do anything bad, just fun." Marcus pulled at Terrence's lunch bag and started to unpack the sandwich Terrence had stuffed back inside.

Chase apparently thought of going a different route in convincing Terrence to help them, and Terrence had to admit he found himself nodding his head as Chase said the words, "Look, we don't want to do anything bad, that's why we need you with us. I know sometimes the Thunder and Lightning can be a bit much. You can help us mellow things out a bit. We have an entire two weeks before this trip, and we need something interesting to pass the time."

Terrence felt himself weakening to the idea. Marcus swooped in to seal the deal. "Besides, the girls are going to assume you were a part of it anyway. You might as well have a say in what happens. If Shar figures it out too quickly or it goes sideways, she is digging three graves, not two!"

Chase took his cue. "And even if they figure out you weren't involved, Akiya's going to ask why you didn't stop us. Either way, bro, you're a part of the club. You might as well embrace the magic."

Terrence pretended to relent. But, in reality, he was kind of already hooked from the start. Talking to his brother earlier that morning had gotten him feeling nostalgic about all the pranks they used to play on each other. He even found himself laughing out loud as he remembered the time he'd asked to play hide-and-seek with Trevor and had found the perfect hiding place—in his brother's closet. He could hear Trevor calling for him, and finally his brother had said he gave up and Terrence could come out because he'd won. Terrence had decided that would be too easy and he'd wanted to see just how long he could successfully hide. To make it even more challenging, he'd burrowed under a pile of clothes in the corner of the closet. The only thing was, the clothes had been so comfy, he'd fallen asleep. And those clothes on top of him had also muffled the sound of his brother calling for him and telling him he really needed to come out because he was worried and he would be calling the police to help search for him. Trevor must have decided to call their mom first, and he'd just been telling her that Terrence must have fallen through a wormhole and was now floating through space when he heard snoring come from his closet. When Trevor recounted the story, he said he thought it was their dog, but when he'd looked over, the dog had been playing with his chew toy on the other side of the room. That was when he looked in the closet, lifted the clothes, and saw Terrence fast asleep. He was so mad that he gently lifted Terrence up and slid him under his parents' bed. When Terrence awoke and realized he was no longer in his brother's closet, he thought he had been transported to another dimension and started screaming until his brother came in laughing. Terrence was now laughing out loud himself.

"Did you think of something good?" asked Marcus.

"Oh, yeah. So, maybe Chase can hack into their phones and change all their playlists when they go to listen to music." Terrence didn't really think this was a good idea, it was just the first thing that popped into his mind.

"Hack into phones? Dude, are you trying to get us on a watch list?"

Marcus followed up with his own idea. "I saw this prank where someone mixed up a bowl of Skittles with M&Ms, so if you put a handful in your mouth, it would be this awful combination and it would take forever to figure out which one was chocolate and which was tangy."

"No can do!" Terrence was surprised he and Chase said this at the same time.

"Jinx, you owe me a soda!" shouted Chase. "Marcus, you know the food rule."

"Oh yeah," said Marcus. "Never lie about what is in food, and you must disclose all ingredients."

The three boys shook their heads in unison remembering the scary time they learned Shar's little brother was in the hospital because someone didn't disclose they used tree nuts in a dish they made. Her little brother was allergic to nuts.

"Okay, no food pranks. Let's use something they are excited about." Marcus sat back in his chair and put on his deep-thinking face, which meant his eyes were closed so tightly his face wrinkled, and his hands were on the back of his head.

"They're excited about visiting the college campus." Terrence couldn't believe he blurted that part out. Now he was definitely all in with the prank. No turning back now.

"That's right!" shouted Chase. "Okay, fellas, I think I have it!"

"So, what's the big plan, my man?" Marcus was smiling so hard Terrence thought the look on his face alone might give things away.

Terrence started to look around the cafeteria to see if he could spot the girls. As he was looking around the room, something red hit the corner of his eye. It was Shar's headband. As he was trying to figure out if the headband was more burgundy than red, Shar must have felt someone looking at her because she turned her head toward Terrence. He turned quickly, then looked back again to see if she was still looking.

She was, along with Ebony and Akiya. Terrence pretended to wave at someone else at the table next to the girls.

"What are you doing?" Chase was looking at Terrence with an expression of confusion.

"I was just making sure the girls weren't close enough to hear us. What's your plan?"

Chase shrugged and started in on the plan. "Well, we know the girls are most excited about going to visit Howard University. What if we played a prank about that? Like maybe send them letters saying they were accepted right now and should be ready to start class while we are on the trip."

"I don't think they would fall for that." Terrence shrugged while taking a big bite of his sandwich that he had for lunch. "I mean, Akiya of all people would know that you have to at least be finished with middle school before you think about starting college. Got anything else?"

"Terrence is right. No way will they think they got accepted into college. But I like where you were going,

Chase. Let me have a crack at it." Marcus was rubbing his hands together and smiling as if he had a really mischievous plan. "My mom and auntie are both members of one of those girl clubs that you see on campus. You know; the ones that all wear the same colors."

"Yeah! My dad is in one, too. He said that's how he and mom met." Chase could hardly stay in his seat.

"A fraternity? My brother joined one last year. I guess the girl groups are called sororities." Terrence's interest was piqued.

"So, let's send the girls postcards saying they got selected to be junior members of some sorority. Those clubs have all kinds of secret handshakes and stuff like that, so the girls just might buy that they have a secret middle school club they never heard of before." Marcus leaned back in his seat, satisfied with his plan.

"Are you sure this won't set Shar off and have her lay a good karate chop on each of us?" Chase looked genuinely concerned; Terrence felt genuinely concerned.

"Don't tell me you're actually scared of her." Marcus was shaking his head.

"Yes, very scared."

"Me too! And don't rule out Akiya and Ebony, they could be hiding a secret wallop as well." Terrence snuck a quick glance in the direction of the table where the girls were sitting.

"Come on, it's a simple prank. We'll tell them it was a joke long before we get to DC. Besides, remember the whole 'too classy to hit people'? If they didn't karate chop Garth when he was trying out his evil villain routine, I'm pretty sure we're safe." Marcus finished up his drink and started cleaning up his area. "Now we just have to get the materials that we need. Terrence, you think you can get your brother to send us some postcards? I want them to look really official!"

Terrence found himself sneaking another peek when he heard his name. "Yeah, sure. I'm pretty sure I have at least three postcards I got from the giftshop when we dropped my brother off at campus last year."

"Well, it doesn't matter if you have three, we need four. Remember, Ebony has two houses. We should send a card to both houses to make sure she gets it on the same day as the other two." Chase was a great planner and was already taking charge of the plan.

"I think I can swing four." Terrence was remembering that he ended up getting five postcards for $10. When he thought about having only one postcard left when this was all over, he thought this might turn out to be a pretty expensive prank. Oh well, it still might be something fun to do to pass the time. Plus, they were going to tell the girls the truth before the trip, so they wouldn't be disappointed with the trip. They would be so excited about going to DC, they might even forget the prank even happened.

Terrence wasn't quite sure he believed that last part. But he did think it was probably a good idea to believe it could happen. Really, this might actually work. It was funny but not too mean. Plus, no one would get hurt. Well, no one would get hurt if they could outrun Shar and Ebony didn't have some big rocket in her backpack that she could launch in their direction. But, most importantly, this prank wasn't bad enough to get them on some government watch list. Well, at least he thought not, or maybe he hoped not.

 Chapter 4

Terrence went straight to his room after school and opened his drawer full of knickknacks he'd picked up on various trips. There were snow globes and pens, buttons and bookmarks, posters and postcards. He loved having reminders of all the places they had visited. They got to travel quite a bit, mainly due to his dad's job. His dad was a part of the Army Corp of Engineers. He went all over the country, and sometimes the world, doing engineering projects; he helped rebuild levees and bridges and even helped on the construction of a new dam in Central America.

Terrence didn't always get a chance to travel with his dad, but he cherished every time he was able to. Mainly, it was projects his dad worked during the summers. Those were the times when having a dad who traveled a lot wasn't so bad. But during the school year, his dad traveled alone. He would be gone for weeks at a time, sometimes even over a month, but he always made sure to call Terrence every night when he was away.

Almost without thinking, Terrence opened the next drawer. This one was filled with knickknacks his dad had picked up for him when Terrence didn't travel with him. It made him feel good to know that his dad was always thinking about him, even when he was away. Soon, his thoughts drifted toward his brother. Trevor always used to be there to help him feel better when his dad was away. Now that he was away at college too, Terrence realized just how alone he could feel sometimes.

His phone ringing startled him out of his thoughts.

"Hey, little brother, what's popping?" Trevor sounded happy and upbeat.

"Not too much, getting some Howard postcards together." Terrence wondered if his brother could tell from his voice that he was missing him.

"Howard postcards, what are you going to do with those?"

Terrence told his brother the plan.

"Are you sure that's a good idea? I don't even know if there is such a thing as a junior sorority." Trevor's voice now sounded more concerned than upbeat.

"Yeah, that's the whole point. It's a prank. Don't worry, we're going to tell the girls it was just a joke way before we leave for DC."

"Dude, you leave for DC in two weeks. You sure that's enough time to write fake postcards, mail them, see the prank unfold, then apologize to the girls? Plus, you want to make sure to give them enough time to forgive you, if they choose to! They might not. And it won't be a very fun trip with three young ladies angry with you, and with good reason."

Terrence shivered a bit then pulled himself together. "The girls aren't like that. They're cool. They'll know it was just a joke."

"Well," his brother began in that big brother tone Terrence wasn't all that fond of, "if they're that cool, are you ready to deal with the revenge that might come back to you? They say karma isn't very much fun. Now, I know you and I have played some pranks on each other, but pranking girls? You might be a little bit out of your league. You sure you want all that smoke?" Trevor was now laughing.

"Oh, I can handle it. I'll just be sure to pack my fire extinguisher."

"Dude, you're asking for smoke with the ladies, you might need more than that. You might need to be wearing a full hazmat suit and have the hospital on speed dial for good measure. But I'll let you and your friends learn the hard way."

The two brothers talked for a few more minutes. Trevor tried one more time to get Terrence to change his mind, but Terrence assured him it was all in good fun. After a couple more jokes, Trevor asking Terrence to bring a watch he had left in his bedroom when they came to DC and Terrence letting his brother know he needed at least two candy bars as payment for acting as a personal delivery driver, the boys ended their phone call.

***

Terrence woke up early the next day to get ready for school. He thought a bit more about the words that his brother had spoken and considered whether this prank would be as innocent as he thought. But he decided that the girls would understand that it was just a joke. This was a good prank, the kind where no one would get hurt. He stuffed the postcards into his backpack and headed downstairs for breakfast.

"Why do you look like that?" asked his mom.

"Like what?" Terrence wished there was a mirror where he could see his face. He thought it looked normal. What did his mom mean?

"I don't know, that weird look you get when you and Trevor are up to something."

Terrence wondered how his mother could read that much into an expression on his face. Did all mothers have this type of ability or did his mom have some sort of superpower? Could dads do this kind of face reading? Wait, was Mrs. Worthington a mother? What about the other teachers at school? Principal Davis? No, that couldn't be right. If all adults could read the faces of all kids, Marcus and Chase wouldn't get a chance to pull half the pranks they pulled. There was a reason they were called Lightning and Thunder.

Marcus and Chase were great friends and so much fun to be around. They were also incredibly smart, so smart that they often had to make up their own things to learn because they would finish their schoolwork so early. And that's when the legendary adventures of Lightning and Thunder were born. They'd started out relatively benign. In elementary school, Marcus and Chase started writing their own comic book. The main characters were superheroes called Lightning and Thunder and they would go on grand adventures. However, the adventures always ended with them leaving a clue that the adventures were real by doing something at their school. It might be moving a trophy from the trophy case and putting it in the third stall of the boys' bathroom or taking all the red crayons out of the crayon boxes and making them form the superheroes' logos they used in the comic. The other kids weren't even upset about their crayons being used. In fact, they were happy to be a part of the comic.

The comic was the coolest thing to happen that entire year at the elementary school. It was so popular, even the kids were reading it. Terrence's brother Trevor would even ask Terrence for his copy every week when he got home from school. That's why Terrence made it his personal mission to figure out who was writing it. He became an expert on the various kids at school with him. While everyone else loved reading the comics, Terrence was most excited about solving the mystery of who the writers might be. He figured out early that there had to be more than one writer. There were two distinct writing and illustration styles. One character talked about computers and sports a lot while the other character talked about gadgets and how to get out of trouble.

After surveying his classmates for a month, Terrence was confident he had figured it out. The writers of the comic had to be cousins Marcus and Chase. He was so curious as to whether he was right, he got the courage to confront them with his thoughts. At first, they denied it, but once Terrence convinced them that their secret was safe with him, they admitted to him their secret identity.

This was the start of Lightning and Thunder transforming from a duo to a trio, at least for some things. Terrence got to get a sneak peek of the comics for the week and sometimes acted as a lookout for Marcus and Chase when they distributed them. Part of the lure was the other kids and teachers not knowing who was writing the comics. It had been an exciting six months. Then the unexpected happened. Marcus and Chase got caught. Well, first they got cocky and decided to go extra big for the last issue of the comic for the school year. They decided to do a more complicated final event that involved the entire school. It was going to take a long time to set up the plan, which included coming to school early to set up a banner in the cafeteria. To make sure they had enough time, they stayed after school and put the comics on students' and teachers' desks so all their time could be spent putting up the banner early the next day. They hadn't planned on a couple of classroom teachers coming back to school that night and finding the comic ahead of time. The teachers were waiting there in the morning when Marcus and Chase showed up to school with the banner. They were caught, but since the banner was just wishing all the kids, teachers, and faculty a good summer, the teachers let them hang it anyway and said they would keep their identity a secret.

Having been unmasked, the cousins decided to discontinue their comic writing. However, they did release a final issue, letting all the kids know they were the writers of the comics. Lightning and Thunder were the stars of the elementary school for an entire day. But Marcus and Chase did something else. They wrote a third character into their comic for that last issue. It was the cool private eye who had uncovered their secret identity. And this private eye didn't even have a secret name; he was identified from the beginning as Terrence. He was later revealed to not just be a private eye but an integral part of keeping the heroes' identity secret from anyone who came close to figuring it out. It was proven in that last comic that Lightning and Thunder had come close to discovery quite a few times, but Private Detective Terrence was always there to throw people off their trail. Why? Because Terrence decided that not only was it important for every town to have a couple of heroes, it was also important for them to have some good, clean fun as well.

Terrence knew Marcus and Chase didn't have to share the limelight that day. But they did. Marcus and Chase were the closest cousins Terrence had ever seen, but they made room in their dynamic duo for him. The only time they left Terrence out was if they thought there might be real trouble. Terrence never thought he would be as close to anyone as he was to his brother. He felt lucky to have Marcus and Chase when his brother left for college. They helped him feel better, and they never told anyone else that he even cried the first day Trevor was gone. He knew Marcus and Chase were great friends, and that was why he felt okay with this prank. Marcus and Chase would never hurt anyone, and neither would Terrence. He was sure the girls would find it funny… eventually.

"Well, I guess you're feeling better now, go ahead and get to school." His mother handed him his lunch bag.

"Wait, my face changed that quickly?"

"Yes, now keep that happy face and not that worried face. Have a good day, and stay out of trouble." His mother gave him a quick hug and kiss on the cheek.

 Chapter 5

When Terrence got to school, he felt like he couldn't get to the classroom fast enough. Marcus and Chase were already sitting at the table behind the bookcase when he came in.

"You got the postcards?" Marcus was smiling like a Cheshire cat.

"Yes, I have them." Terrence pulled the cards from his backpack. "Are you two sure about this?"

"Of course we're sure. This is going to be epic!" Chase was opening his notebook frantically. "I was asking my mom about sororities last night. At first, she thought I was trying to join one myself and started to tell me I might want to look at fraternities. But I told her it was strictly for research purposes. Apparently, there is this thing called the Divine Nine, which is all the historically Black Greek organizations."

"Greek? Like those myths Ebony is always telling us about? What are they, the Zeus's and Athena's clubs or something like that?" Marcus was looking confused.

"Dude, your parents are in a fraternity and sorority, and you know they don't belong to a Zeus club!" Chase was shaking his head.

"Yeah, but you're talking about divination and number nines and all that sort of stuff. I'm confused now!"

"No, it's the Divine Nine, that just means there are nine historically Black fraternities and sororities. While others might be at a historically Black college like Howard, we know the Divine Nine will probably be there. For sororities, there are Alpha Kappa Alpha, Delta Sigma Theta, Zeta Phi Beta, and Sigma Gamma Rho."

"Well, those all sound hard to spell." Terrence craned his neck to try to get a better look at the paper

Chase was reading from. "Let's pick the one that sounds easiest. That Alpha one has the same word twice, I choose that one."

"No, we have to split them up. Let's pick one of each." Marcus pulled the notebook closer to him, apparently to get a better look for himself.

"Would friends go into different sororities though?" asked Terrence. He thought friends might want to belong to the same group. But he wasn't quite sure what went on in a sorority, so maybe it didn't matter.

"No, you can still be friends with people even if they belong to a different sorority. Our moms are twins, and one belongs to Alpha Kappa Alpha and the other belongs to Delta Sigma Theta.

"That's cool. Well, let's choose those two and one more. What was the next one on the list?"

Chase looked at the list again. "Zeta Phi Beta."

"Alright, we put each of the girls in one of those. I'll do Shar and Alpha Kappa Alpha because Shar and

Alpha are the easiest to spell from that list." Terrence was laughing and grabbing a postcard.

"Fine, I'll do Akiya and put her in Delta Sigma Theta." Chase grabbed a card.

"Hey, you all left me with the most work!" Marcus was looking back and forth at Terrence and Chase and wagging his finger. "She has two houses, so I have to write both cards to make sure she gets at least one of them at the exact same time the other two get theirs!"

"I'll write her other one, just to prove what an amazingly awesome, extraordinary human I am." Chase plucked one of the two cards Marcus was holding from his hands.

"So, what should these things say?" Terrence realized he wasn't quite sure what to write as he sat with his pencil ready to begin.

"Let's just say the sorority heard they were coming to Howard and they wanted to welcome them to be junior members. Don't write too much, we don't want to tip them off." Marcus confidently started writing.

"We definitely can't write too much, since we don't know very much about sororities anyway." Terrence now wondered if this would really work after all.

"Less talking, more writing. We have to get these done so I can run to the mailbox on the corner and get them into the mail before the girls get here." Chase had his head down as he spoke, having already started writing.

Before long, all four postcards were complete. Chase put stamps on them he had gotten from his mother. They couldn't decide how many stamps they needed so put three stamps on each postcard just to be safe. Marcus ended up being the one to run the postcards to the mailbox. This was only after he beat Chase in best out of three sprints down the hall to prove who was fastest. Terrence thought this wasted precious time since the girls would be arriving to school with the other students soon, and Mrs. Worthington was starting to get suspicious as to why the boys had gotten to school so early when they didn't have a project to work on. She raised her eyebrows ever so slightly when they mentioned being so excited about the Washington, DC trip that they'd decided to do some extra studying on the nation's capital.

Marcus was off to the mailbox, exclaiming as he left the building that he didn't even know why Chase tried since he was Lightning, after all. "See, Thunder comes after lightning because lightning is so fast and awesome." He did break into an even faster run as Chase pretended to start running after him.

While they had a minute alone, Terrence asked Chase, "So, you really think this is going to work?"

"Sure. Plus, if not, at least we will die together!"

Terrence couldn't figure out if this was all that reassuring. But there wasn't much time to ponder, the other kids had started arriving, and he could see Akiya's head above the crowd. Even though he couldn't see Ebony and Shar yet, he was pretty sure they were with her.

***

Terrence couldn't believe how fast the mail delivery was. Just two days later, Shar, Ebony, and Akiya were running into the classroom to show the boys their postcards. Terrence felt his stomach drop. He guessed he was going to see if his brother was right or if he really was ready for the smoke that was to follow.

Akiya was talking so fast he could hardly follow her. "I've been invited to be a junior member of Delta Sigma Theta! Oh my gosh, this is so awesome. I didn't even realize it would be this amazing until I got the postcard. I don't know how they even heard about me. But isn't this cool?"

Marcus smiled widely and said, "Real cool. What about you, Shar? Delta Sigma Theta for you too?"

"Nope, Alpha Kappa Alpha for me! I saw their colors were pink and green, don't you think that suits me? I love pink. I love green." Shar pointed to those two colors on her jacket.

"You love all colors, Shar. Even in that jacket, you have about every color the rainbow can produce." Chase reached out to touch her jacket.

"You can look at the awesomeness, just don't touch." Shar pulled her jacket more tightly around her before Chase could reach it.

Terrence steadied himself and asked as innocently as possible, "What about you, Ebony?"

"Zeta Phi Beta." Her voice had a weird inflection as if she was trying to hold back some of her excitement. "They wanted me so badly, they sent me two postcards, one to castle one and one to castle two. I thought that was pretty neat." As Ebony spoke those words, something in her eyes flashed a bit. Terrence wasn't sure, but it seemed as if something just came to her mind, and now she looked as if she was thinking really hard.

Chase must have spotted the same thing because he said, "Look at the time, boys, we better run!" He took off down the hall, proving that he could run just as fast as Marcus with the right motivation.

Akiya may have been having the same thought as Ebony because she looked at Shar as Terrence was walking away and said, "Let me see your postcard."

***

Terrence didn't have to wait long to see what the end result of those reflections might be. By lunchtime, the boys pretty much knew they were toast, mainly because the three girls made a beeline to where the boys were sitting and pretending to read.

Shar was the first to speak, but her eyes told Terrence everything he needed to know; this was not going to be a pleasant conversation. "Did you three really think you were going to get away with this?"

Marcus looked up from the book he was pretending to read and feigned surprise. "Oh, hello, Shar! You're looking well today. Anything new to report?"

Chase let out a noise that vacillated between amusement and terror. He looked over to Akiya and managed to say, ever so quietly, "Did you get mail?"

Akiya glared at Chase then Marcus. "Oh yeah, we got mail alright. And I just want to point out this little thing called mail fraud."

Terrence let out an accidental yelp. His heart was racing, and thoughts spun around in his head. Could their prank really have broken a law?

"See, boy—" Ebony took a deep breath as if she was trying to calm herself down "—you can't just stick whatever you want into a mailbox and put a stamp on it, pretending that it is official when it isn't. I wonder how many years they'll put you three in jail for. Ten, twenty, fifty!"

Shar was now grinning like an alchemist that who learned to turn rocks into gold. "Imagine going to jail before high school." She turned to see Terrence pushing his lunch bag away from himself. "Oh no, don't stop eating on my account, it just might be your last good meal."

Marcus looked at Chase and Terrence and yelled, "Run for it, boys!"

Akiya caught him before he completed his first step. Terrence admired the way she was so graceful in using her height to her advantage. He could remember when she was one of the shortest people in their classroom, but she had grown quite a few inches in the last couple of years.

"Terrence, what in the world are you gawking at? We're not really going to send you three to jail."

Terrence started. Why did he keep forgetting he was looking at people when he got lost in his thoughts?

"No jail? That's a relief." Chase sank back into his chair and grabbed his lunch.

"Oh, that doesn't mean you won't be punished, because, believe me, you will be punished. You just won't get the relief that being locked in a cell away from me might afford you." Ebony cracked a half smile and an eyebrow twitch that made the hair on the back of Terrence's neck stand up.

"Wait one minute, young lady," Marcus said bravely, which Terrence thought was insane, waving his finger. "What happened to being too classy for violence? You didn't even deck Garth at Space Camp!"

"Who said anything about violence, Marcus?" Now Shar was sounding so calm, Terrence wondered if violence might be better.

"Absolutely no violence, boy, but believe me; the punishment will definitely fit the crime." Akiya started cracking her knuckles.

Terrence thought he might faint.

"So, how did you three figure it out?" Realizing he wasn't going to jail and wouldn't be pummeled in the middle of the lunchroom, Chase now seemed to want to know where the plan had failed.

"**Bessie Blount Griffin**." Ebony stopped as if saying this name was supposed to answer the question Chase had asked. The look on Marcus' face told Terrence he was thinking the same thing.

"And, what about **Bessie Blount Griffin**? Does she work at the post office or something?" Marcus took a huge bite of his turkey and jelly sandwich as if anticipating a really good story.

"No, silly, **Bessie Blount Griffin** was the first American woman, an African American woman I might add, to be admitted as a student to the Document Division of the Metropolitan Police Forensic Science Laboratory in London, you know—Scotland Yard!"

When Akiya spoke those last words, Chase perked up. "No way, you mean like Sherlock Holmes' Scotland Yard?"

"Even better. Because before she was even accepted there, she was here in the United States working in forensics as a chief examiner for police departments in Virginia. She even used her training to study pre-Civil War documents and had her own private practice. She is the absolute queen of American document forensics, and we used some of her techniques to figure you out!" Ebony put her hands on her hips, clearly excited about this triumph.

"No way! I've heard of computer forensics, but I didn't know about document forensics. So, what did you all do to figure us out? What gave us away?" Chase pulled out a chair for Ebony to sit down. Marcus went and got two more chairs from another table for Akiya and Shar.

 Chapter 6

"Well, the first thing you three did wrong was overplay your hand. Not many people know about castle one and castle two. So, the fact that Ebony got two letters instead of just one was a pretty big giveaway." Shar then helped herself to a few of Chase's potato chips.

"Yeah, that is what got me thinking. Usually for school-related things, mail only comes to castle one, and since this is a school-related event, I should have only gotten mail at castle one."

"I saw your face when you came to that realization." Terrence's heart had stopped racing and he was ready to fully join the conversation. He thought back to when he saw the girls in the hallway with their postcards and could almost see a thought bubble appear above Ebony's head when she mentioned getting two postcards.

"The next clue," began Akiya, "was the number of stamps."

"Did we not put enough?" asked Marcus.

"Literally the opposite; postcards cost less to mail than letters. One stamp would have been plenty, and anyone who actually mails things would have known that."

"We failed you, **Mr. Philip B. Downing**." Marcus hung his head in shame.

Philip B. Downing was the African American inventor the STEAM Chasers had learned about during their scavenger hunt. He holds a patent for the modern-day letter box, the one that the mailbox Marcus had put the postcards in was based off of.

"Any other clues?" Terrence was not equally interested in where their prank went wrong.

Ebony looked at him and gave a laugh as if the list was too long to mention, but she did throw out some additional things. Like that fact that when they started to get suspicious about the letters, they did a web search and couldn't find any junior sororities at Howard University. They also thought the handwriting looked a little too familiar.

"Wait, you can't tell me that you all actually know our handwriting." Marcus sat back in his chair and folded his arms.

Shar snorted. "Chase did Akiya's and one of Ebony's; Marcus wrote the other one for Ebony, namely the one that went to castle two, and Terrence wrote mine."

"She's a witch!" Chase shouted, way too loudly.

"No, I'm not! You just have sloppy handwriting. And Terrence writes his a's two different ways in the same word, and Marcus was in such a rush, he left out the last two words that were on all the other postcards."

"Busted!" Marcus seemed more proud than annoyed. "Besides, maybe we weren't trying to prank you; maybe we were trying to get your investigative juices pumping before our trip to Washington, DC.

You all like schoolwork, and learning about **Bessie Blount Giffin** was good, right? Really, the report just writes itself. You all should be thanking us!"

"Oh, we'll thank you all right." Shar grabbed another handful of chips and got up from the table. Ebony and Akiya joined her, and they walked across the lunchroom and out the door.

"Where do you think they're going?" asked Marcus.

"To plan our demise." Terrence was sure of it.

He had to admit he was pretty impressed that Shar knew he wrote his a's differently within the same word. That was actually a spelling trick he'd learned from his dyslexia tutor when he was younger. He would sometimes get confused about how to write words that had multiple vowels, so for words like banana, if he wrote each *a* differently, he could just focus on how many different ways he wrote the letter *a,* and that would give him a good reminder about how to spell the word. He had used that technique so much that he now wrote all words like that, even ones he could spell easily. He did it for all vowels he wrote, but the *a*'s were the most noticeable. He wondered if Ebony used that trick too. Maybe not, since Shar thought it was unique to him. He needed to remember to ask Ebony what her spelling tricks were, she seemed to be a great speller even though she was dyslexic as well.

Chase pulled Terrence out of his thoughts. "Well, no need to worry about that. They found out pretty quickly, so I'm sure they aren't even that upset. Now, let's head to the library, I want to do some studying on **Bessie Blunt Griffin**. She seems pretty awesome!"

"Are you sure you're not just going to study how to get around written forensics next time?" Marcus grabbed the scraps of his lunch to deposit into the trashcan on their way out.

Terrence grabbed his backpack and headed out with Chase and Marcus. "How about we just admit defeat and chalk this one up to experience?"

At the same time, without even looking at each other or missing a step, Marcus and Chase said, "Never!"

Terrence was surprised to get a text from Chase at 6:00 the next morning. He was calling an emergency meeting of the STEAM Chasers before school. If it was Marcus who had sent the message, he wouldn't have been as concerned. Marcus thought everything just might be an emergency, and Terrence wouldn't think it was an extreme emergency unless Marcus did something strange, like have one of his drones deliver the message. But Chase tended to be more practical. He was also surprised that Chase was asking for all six of the STEAM Chasers to meet in the morning and not just him and Marcus. He wondered what exactly it could be. He was so anxious, in fact, that he never even went back to sleep after getting the text. He didn't quite know how early Chase wanted to get together, so he crawled out of bed and started getting ready for school.

Terrence could already hear his mother downstairs in the kitchen. He had no idea what time his mom got up in the morning, but it always seemed to be before that, especially when his father was away on business.

After getting ready for school, Terrence grabbed his backpack and went downstairs.

"Can't talk, Mom, Chase texted us to meet him early for an emergency meeting of The STEAM Chasers!"

"Sounds serious." His Mom tilted her head to the side as she spoke, as if wanting him to give her more details. "At least let me fix you some toast before you go."

Terrence was about to say no thank you, but his stomach started growling before he could get the words out. He just shrugged his shoulders instead, and his mom laughed while putting two pieces of bread in the toaster. Terrence went to the fridge to grab butter and jam for his toast. He decided to make himself a toast sandwich so he could eat it while he walked to school.

Eating while he walked was a good idea, because it helped him keep his mind off of worrying too much about what Chase might want to talk to them about. He really didn't have a clue.

"So, what do you think this is about?"

Terrence turned to see Akiya catching up to him quickly. Her long legs made her seem to glide rather than walk.

"I have no idea," answered Terrence honestly.

"Well, it better be real good, his text at 6:00 this morning scared me!"

"Were you asleep, too?" Terrence thought that might be a stupid question, of course Akiya was sleep at 6:00 in the morning.

"No, I was reading." She continued, probably seeing the look of shock on Terrence's face, "I read at that time because it is usually quiet in the house. I'm used to hearing nothing but the birds, definitely not my phone. I jumped so high I nearly knocked my chair over!

Terrence felt relieved that he wasn't the only person who'd startled from Chase's mysterious text. He started to wonder again just what Chase had to tell them. He and Akiya walked into the school and toward the classroom together. They met up with Shar and Ebony.

"Terrence, do you have any idea what Chase could want?" Shar was half talking and half yawning. She must have been as sleep as he'd been when she got the text.

Thankfully, they didn't have to wait long to find out.

"What took you all so long?" Marcus looked up from the table as if he had been sitting there all night.

"So long? It's 7:00, school doesn't start for another forty-five minutes. Besides, Chase didn't tell us what time to come, he just said come early." Ebony put her bookbag on the floor. Terrence knew she hated being late to things, but could one really be late to something that didn't have an actual start time?

"Okay, Chase, start talking." Shar grabbed the seat next to Chase and took out her notebook.

"I have uncovered a crime."

Terrence looked around, certainly there had to be more to that statement. If Chase had discovered a crime, why call them and not the police. Ebony clearly had the same thought.

"Chase, if you saw a crime, call the cops. At least call Officer Mitchell or Officer Carpenter. And, if you don't want to call the police, at least tell your parents."

It seemed like Ebony was going to continue with the list of all the people Chase should have called instead of them, but Chase interrupted.

"Not that kind of crime, a cybercrime!"

"Okay, so that would mean you should call the FBI, or at least the Federal Communications Commission, I think they are responsible for the internet. Or would that be the Department of Defense?" Akiya started to grab her tablet, "Let me see which place we should start with first."

"Please don't get me involved with anything that has to do with the FBI. My mom used to watch Criminal Minds, the FBI deals with serial killers! I do not want to be involved with anyone who is also involved with serial killers. Chase, what have you gotten us mixed up in!" The look on Shar's face told

Terrence she was already thinking about being chased through the streets by some masked clown or werewolf. Shar hated being scared, and whenever she saw a scary movie, she thought werewolves or killer clowns were the next reasonable step in the situation.

"Guys, this isn't about serial killers or the FBI." Chase was trying to win back the group and calm everyone down. Akiya, you already have your tablet, do me a favor. Look up **Bessie Blount Griffin**."

"Why do I have to look her up, we already studied her?" Akiya protested.

"Just humor me, please? Look her up and get her picture ready."

Akiya complied and placed her tablet in the middle of the table.

"Okay, now, Ebony, take your tablet and look up **Marie Van Brittan Brown** and place her picture on the table."

Ebony looked at Chase, surprised. "She invented the security system, she didn't work in forensic analysis. Why are we looking her up?"

74

"Humor me, please!"

Ebony placed her tablet on the table with the picture showing.

"What in the world? **Marie Van Brittan Brown** had a double identity?" Marcus grabbed the tablets, looking back and forth at each picture.

"No, she didn't have a double identity," Chase looked serious, "that isn't it at all."

"Oh, were they twins? That's pretty cool, it's sort of like yours and Marcus's moms are twins." Terrence grabbed the tablets from Marcus. It was uncanny. Even though Chase and Marcus's Moms were twins, they still had enough distinctive features where you could tell them apart. There was virtually no difference between the two pictures he was looking at.

"No, Terrence, they aren't identical twins. **Marie Van Brittan Brown** was born in 1922, while **Bessie Blount Griffin** was born in 1914."

"Wait," Shar said hesitantly, "I don't understand. These look like the same picture. If they weren't twins and they weren't the same person, what is going on?"

"That's the mystery. I went home to study **Bessie Blount Griffin** and learn about some of the techniques you all were telling us about. When I saw the picture, it seemed like I had seen it somewhere before. Then, I remembered when we were at Ebony's house and learned about **Marie Van Brittan Brown**. So, I looked her up, and there it was, the exact same picture staring back at me."

"But how?" Akiya asked the question everyone else seemed to be thinking.

"That, my friends, is the mystery. That is what The STEAM Chasers have to discover."

Terrence looked around the table at his friends, this really was an emergency important enough to wake everyone up at 6:00 in the morning.

As they sat around the table and searched the internet, they slowly started to figure out what must have happened. Somewhere, at some time, the famous picture that showed up for both women was correctly identified as one, but incorrectly identified as the other. It had been that way online for so long, it seemed almost impossible to figure out which was the correct picture.

"Even if we think we figured it out, what do we do?" asked Akiya solemnly.

"I have it!" Marcus banged the table in a way that gave Terrence a jolt, "We're going to the National Museum of African American History and Culture in a couple of weeks, certainly the museum should be able to help."

"That's a great idea!" Chase gave Marcus a high five.

"In the meantime, let's get to work trying to figure out whom this picture actually belongs to and what the actual picture should be for the other person. They deserve to have their own identity, the right identity." Terrence wasn't sure what came over him, but he felt it was his mission to help right this wrong.

"What's wrong, Ebony?" Akiya looked across the table, and Ebony had dropped her head into her hands.

"I just had a thought, what if both pictures are wrong?"

"Well, we'll just have to hope that isn't the case. If anyone can figure it out, we can!" Marcus gave Ebony a high five. Just as they finished, the other students started piling into the room.

 Chapter 7

Three days later, Terrence was again awoken from his sleep by his phone. He looked to see who was calling and got excited. "Hey, Trevor!"

"Well, I guess you survived the great prank. How did it go?"

Terrence told his brother all about how the girls had figured things out so quickly using written forensics.

"I figured you all wouldn't be able to fool them for long. Have they gotten you back yet?"

Terrence was surprised by this question. "What do you mean?"

"I mean three smart girls who got pranked by their friends. You said they took it in good stride; that makes me feel like they may have a little something planned for you all in return."

"No way!" Terrence replied with less confidence than he had hoped.

"Well, don't say I didn't warn you," replied his brother. "Anyway, let your friends know we have some really cool things planned for them. It should be educational, even for the amazing STEAM Chasers."

"I'm counting on it!" Terrence could feel the smile on his face as he talked. The conversation went on for about ten more minutes, then Trevor needed to get off the phone and head to class. Terrence looked at the clock and realized he needed to start getting ready for school as well.

**

When he got to school, he met Marcus and Chase and told them about his brother's warning.

"No way will they try to get us back. Besides, if they were planning something, they would have done it by now," Marcus said confidently.

"They can't still be mad at me; I got us a mystery to solve." Chase folded his arms, clearly feeling confident that he was safe from further pranking.

"I think we're okay. Well, at least I hope we're okay."

"Terrence, my man." Marcus put his arm around Terrence's shoulder as he talked. "I know this is your first big time school prank, but we got your back. You will be a pro at this in no time."

Chase was on his other side and gave him a pat on the back. "Welcome to the dark side, my brother. Shar may have wanted a bit of revenge in the beginning, but I'm sure Akiya and Ebony talked her down. They're probably laughing about it as we speak."

Just when Terrence was starting to feel confident, he started off down the hall and saw Akiya, Ebony, and Shar speaking with Principal Davis. His heart stopped.

"Are they telling on us?" he asked Marcus and Chase.

"No way." Marcus tried to sound reassuring.

Shar must have felt their eyes on her because she looked around and stared directly at Terrence. She had an expression on her face that Terrence couldn't quite read. This made him even more nervous because he thought he knew all of Shar's facial expressions.

By the time they reached Principal Davis and the others, they were finishing up their conversation.

"Don't worry, ladies," Terrence heard Principal Davis say, "we'll take care of it."

Terrence wondered if he should start running right then and there. However, Principal Davis turned and gave him, Chase, and Marcus a smile. He then patted Marcus and Chase on the back and said, "I hope you all are looking forward to the trip. It is going to be great."

"Yes, sir!" said Chase.

Terrence couldn't speak. He wasn't sure what the appropriate response might be. Did Principal Davis know about the prank? He couldn't even read Akiya's or Ebony's face, and that made him even more nervous.

Principal Davis bounded down the hall, adjusting his tie that Terrence could see was decorated with puppies riding sharks that were somehow playing guitars. He had no idea where Principal Davis could possibly be getting his ties.

"So," Terrence heard Chase saying in what appeared to be an overly sweet voice, "what was Principal Davis taking care of for you three?"

"Nosey much?" asked Shar.

"No, not nosey. Curious. Concerned. Inquisitive." Chase seemed to be trying to find another word.

"Nosey," said Ebony matter-of-factly.

"It was something about our trip to Washington, DC. Any other questions, or are we free to go to class?" Akiya had a half smile on her face as she talked, which made Terrence a bit unsure if that was the entire story. Before he could think of what to do next, Chase jumped in.

"No, you can't go to class yet. Did anyone find information on our mystery?"

"Oh, I did!" said Akiya as she put her book bag on the floor and pulled out a folder. "I printed these last night." They looked to be old newspaper articles. "I can't believe how hard it was to find pictures online of people who were alive not that long ago. I could find pictures of people who passed away an even longer time ago, like **Dr. Martin Luther King Junior** or **Malcolm X** and even **Rosa Parks**. For the life of me, I can't figure out why it was so hard to hunt down a picture of **Marie Van Brittan Brown** and **Bessie Blount Griffin**. But I do think I solved part of the mystery. I ran it by Ebony, and she agreed."

Akiya handed everyone pieces of paper that had a picture she'd printed off the internet. It was a picture of a man and woman.

Terrence saw the drawing next to the picture. "Hey, this is a patent picture of the video security system **Marie Van Brittan Brown** and her husband designed."

"Exactly," replied Ebony. "And that picture is of **Marie Van Brittan Brown** and her husband, **Albert**

Brown. As you can see, that picture doesn't resemble the identical picture that we saw. So, using some of **Bessie Blount Griffin's** techniques, we're pretty sure that picture is not **Marie Van Britton Brown**. Now we just have to confirm that the picture is actually **Bessie Blount Griffin**."

"Wow! This is great!" Chase gave Ebony and Akiya a high five.

"Hey, man, you got some face recognition software you can run these pictures through, just to be doubly sure?" asked Marcus.

"I can try, but it might not be easy. Did you know a lot of facial recognition software can't accurately identify African Americans and other darker-skinned people? That's probably why these pictures got mixed up in the first place."

"And why you better get busy developing some technology that actually works for us." Shar put her hands on her hips as she spoke.

Terrence saw Chase start to blush. He knew Chase loved when people recognized how good he was at computer programming. He was a Python expert and was even developing his own apps. If anyone could develop good facial recognition software, it would be Chase.

Akiya looked at her watch. "Well, now do we have permission to get to class, Chase? I don't want to be late."

"Permission granted, Princess Akiya," Chase said with a smile.

"Or should that be queen?" asked Marcus. "I never know how much royal we are putting on Akiya at any given time. You don't want to demote the monarch; it might be 'off with your head'!"

"Ha-ha," said Akiya as she grabbed her backpack, and they all headed to class.

 Chapter 8

The next week and a half flew by so quickly, Terrence could hardly believe it. Now he found himself looking at a packing list and double-checking that he had everything. Remembering what happened on their way to Space Camp, he made sure he had lots of underwear. Marcus had already texted him five times trying to get him to reveal everything that Trevor was going to do with them on the tour. But Terrence had promised his brother that he would make sure to leave some secrets so his friends would have some nice surprises.

"Terrence, hurry up! We need to get going to the airport," Terrence's Mom called from downstairs.

Terrence didn't know if it was a good or a bad thing that his mom was going to be one of the chaperones for the trip to DC. He guessed it didn't matter too much since his brother would be doing the tour as well. It would be a family reunion of sorts. Too bad his dad was deployed. Something about needing to rebuild a bridge somewhere that had collapsed due to a storm. Those sorts of calls weren't that bad, it usually only meant his dad would be gone for a few weeks. He should be getting back sometime soon.

His dad didn't actually have to build the bridge himself. He was a civil engineer for the Army Corps of Engineers. That meant his job was to review the plans the architectural, mechanical, and structural engineers had put together for the new bridge. He would also suggest changes that could be made so that the bridge would work better for the community. Oftentimes, how people live and work changes over time, and a bridge that has worked well for twenty or thirty years doesn't work as well anymore. It wasn't a good thing that the bridge became unstable, but at least something sort of good could happen after the storm.

Terrence took one last look in his bag and headed downstairs. It was a quick ride to the airport, where they parked on the third level of the parking deck. They had barely gotten their bags out of the trunk when he heard his name.

"Hey, Terrence! Wait up!"

He looked around and saw Marcus and Chase heading toward him.

"Perfect timing, am I right?" Marcus was looking at his watch. He loved being extremely organized whenever he was traveling. Terrence figured it was because Marcus was used to following flight plans. When he flew his drone at really high altitudes, sometimes he had to get special permission. This was one of the reasons he needed to get a drone license and made local history being the youngest person in his town to earn one.

"This trip is going to be awesome, starting with the plane ride. I hope I'm sitting by the window." Chase was looking up as he talked, as if he could already see the clouds they would be flying through.

"Well, hopefully we are all sitting together. If I'm seated by the window, I'll make sure to switch with you, I don't mind at all." Terrence was starting to feel more excited. The thought of them being able to sit together on the plane was intriguing.

"Yeah, I looked up the plane we are taking, and it is a cool one with three seats on each side. Too bad we don't know our seat assignments yet though."

Chase clearly wasn't going to let anything take away his enthusiasm. "I'm sure they made sure to sit us all together. All the adults will probably want to cluster together anyway. They'll be stuck with us for five days straight; they know we can't get into that much trouble on an airplane."

Terrence hoped Chase was right.

Marcus lifted his head a bit as they got closer to the airport's entrance. "Hey, it's Principal Davis and Mrs. Worthington. And I see some kids from our class as well. They look like they are handing out tickets to people. Let's run to catch up."

"Not so fast, young men." Terrence's mom came up behind them. "Marcus and Chase, I told your moms they could go ahead and beat traffic on their way back into the city. So I'm officially on chaperone duty as of right now. The last thing I need is for one of you to be hit by a freight train running across the street."

Chase and Marcus started to laugh under their breath. They weren't being mean to Terrence; they knew all too well what it was like having a parent chaperone.

Terrence looked at his mom. "Freight train, Mom? At an airport? With no train tracks for miles?"

"Exactly. A chaperone is always expecting the unexpected. You would be surprised by all the things that I see come across my desk that no one expected. Remember that time I told you about the guy who was hit by a plane jogging on the beach? Didn't even see it coming because he was wearing headphones and didn't hear that engine roaring behind him. I bet if you told him the day before that someone could get hit by a plane on a beach, he would have told you that wasn't likely either. Well, now we both know different."

"Your mom has the coolest stories!" Marcus gave Terrence a pat on the back.

"I could listen to stories of unexpected death and destruction all day." Chase now had a weird smile on his face.

Terrence usually relayed the really weird stories back to Marcus and Chase. His mother was an actuary for an insurance company. This meant that she used lots of math and statistics to figure out risks. This job helped insurance companies figure out how much to charge people to make sure they didn't go broke paying out lots of polices on people getting hit by planes jogging down the beach.

They walked the rest of the way so as not to make Terrence's mom too nervous. Ebony and Akiya waved them over as they walked through the doors.

"Hey, guys!" she said excitedly. "Grab your tickets from Principal Davis. We're going to get through security so we can stop and buy some snacks before we get on the plane."

"We don't need too many snacks though," added Akiya, "this plane ride is only about an hour long. We have a layover in Atlanta before we get to Washington, DC."

The three boys headed over to get their tickets. Shar was just getting hers from Mrs. Worthington and gave the boys a smile.

"What was that for?" asked Chase.

Shar just shrugged her shoulders.

They made their way to Principal Davis.

"Ebony said we should get our ticket from you, Principal Davis," said Chase.

"Oh yes, I've got you three all taken care of. Here you go." Principal Davis handed each of them a folder.

They said thank you and headed back over toward the girls.

"I wonder what he meant by he had us three all taken care of," Terrence wondered out loud.

"Probably nothing. All I heard was snacks. Let's get in the security line." Marcus was already heading toward the sign pointing them to the security entrance.

It wasn't too bad going through security, and they were quickly in the terminal where their plane would be departing. They stopped by a small store where everyone loaded up with water, candy bars, and chips.

'Hey, I just heard them say they were going to start boarding our plane in ten minutes, let's get to our gate." Marcus led the way as they headed to their gate.

With all the familiar faces, Terrence thought it felt more like the school cafeteria than an airport. It looked like the entire school was going to DC.

Backpacks ready, it was time to board the plane. This was the first time Terrence, Marcus, and Chase looked at their tickets.

"What seat are you in, Chase?" asked Marcus.

"I'm in seat A," said Chase. "What about you, Terrence?"

Terrence looked at his ticket. "I'm in seat B."

"Sweet!" said Marcus. "I'm in seat C."

"What row are you in?" asked Terrence, remembering the other important part of a seat assignment.

"Row eight," answered Chase.

"Me too," said Marcus.

"I'm in row nine."

"So, you're in the middle, but not in our row? I wonder who is sitting between us and who you're in between.

The three of them found out very quickly who they were seated with and why. Principal Davis was the one to let them know. "Hey, guys, I want you to know what good friends you have in Shar, Ebony, and Akiya. They quietly told me the three of you are a bit worried about flying. So, to make the flight not so bad, I put Marcus and Chase in the row with me. Terrence, you will be with your mom and Mrs. Worthington. The rest of the kids will all be together a little further back on the plane, so don't worry about anyone seeing you if you get a little scared."

Terrence couldn't tell if the look on Marcus's face was more shock or indignation. Marcus being afraid to fly was the most preposterous thing he had ever heard. Marcus talked about wanting to get his pilot's license before his driver's license. But Terrence didn't have time to feel sorry for Marcus; he was feeling sorry for himself having to sit between his mother and Mrs. Worthington. They were actually good friends and would probably be talking the entire time. It was his mother who'd first volunteered his big brother to get a tour together for his class. Thankfully, Trevor decided to make it the most epic tour possible. Terrence looked over to see how Chase was taking the news of having to ride in the plane next to Principal Davis; he saw Chase shaking his head in disbelief.

Shar walked past and whispered just loud enough for the three of them to hear, "Have a good flight, boys."

"Oh, they're good. They are very good." Marcus was looking at Akiya and Ebony as he spoke. The two of them could clearly see the boys had just been told of their seating assignments.

"Well, I guess they won," said Terrence, a bit relieved that that pranking could be over.

"Oh, no, we're just getting started." Marcus was rubbing his hands together.

The only thing Chase could mutter was, "It's on."

 Chapter 9

Terrence decided the best plan of action was to close his eyes and try to go to sleep. He found his eyelids getting tired to the sounds of his mother and Mrs. Worthington trying to remember the name of some soul food restaurant they loved to visit whenever they were in Washington, DC. He drifted off with the two women talking about all of the savory food they couldn't wait to have when they stopped by Henry's Soul Café and their excitement about trying some of the restaurants they'd heard about that were located inside the National Museum of African American History and Culture.

Terrence bolted upright when he heard his name.

"Are you listening to this, Terrence? Wake up! You're missing it!"

Terrence finally realized it was Chase who had been calling his name.

"Dude, Principal Davis has all the details! This is awesome!" Marcus had joined in the idea of waking Terrence up by talking as loud as possible.

Terrence leaned forward in his seat and saw Principal Davis on his cell phone.

"Principal Davis, do you ever stop working?" Terrence asked with a laugh.

"Oh no, Terrence. This isn't work, this is fun. I was getting Marcus and Chase ready for our layover in Atlanta. You know Hartsfield-Jackson Atlanta International Airport is one of the busiest airports in the world, right?"

Terrence nodded his head. He only knew that because it was one of the facts that was listed in a booklet for his Boeing 757 aircraft model he'd put together the previous year.

"Well, I heard the captain say the name of the terminal we are going to be stopping at for our quick layover, and it is the nearest one to the international terminal, so I got excited. I remembered some information that might be pretty exciting for the STEAM Chasers."

"You won't believe this!" Marcus shouted. He clearly couldn't wait for Principal Davis to finish his story.

"Well, I happen to know that the international terminal was built by several companies, one of which was C.D. Moody Construction. They are an African American owned construction company that did a lot of important work on the international terminal, including constructing an underground connector to an existing concourse and doing some tunnel extensions and new station facilities for the Automatic People Mover. The owner of the company, **C. David Moody Jr.**, is an amazing man. He even graduated from Howard University."

"Hey!" said Terrence, feeling himself wake up fully with excitement, "I know what that is! That's the subway thing you get to ride from terminal to terminal!"

Mrs. Worthington was now joining the conversation. "I had no idea a Black American owned construction company had done some of the work on that terminal. I was there last winter when I took a trip to Senegal."

"I didn't know either." Terrence's mom was now leaning forward in her chair as well. "Terrence, did you know who the international terminal was named for in Atlanta?"

"Um, no," answered Terrence, grimacing with the thought that he probably should have known the answer to that question.

"I know!" a voice from about three rows behind them called out. "Sorry, I heard STEAM Chasers and it got my attention! The terminal is known as the Maynard Jackson International Terminal, named after **Maynard Holbrook Jackson, Jr.**, the first Black mayor in Atlanta, Georgia."

"And why do you know that, Akiya?" Chase asked. Terrence couldn't tell if Chase was more amazed or flabbergasted by Akiya's ability to know so many facts.

"I knew we had a layover in Atlanta, so I decided to do some reading about the airport, it got exciting. But I didn't know that an African American construction company had helped to build the terminal named after **Mayor Jackson**. That is pretty awesome."

"So, the only person who knows something Akiya doesn't know is the principal of a school. Makes sense." Chase shrugged his shoulders and sat back in his chair.

"Oh yes, but just wait until we get ready to land in our final stop of Washington, DC. I have something pretty exciting to tell you about that airport as well!"

Changing planes went by quickly, and before they all knew it, they were on the last leg of their journey to Washington, DC.

"Okay, we're getting ready to land, Principal Davis, what big thing did you want to tell us about this airport?" Marcus asked as he pulled his chair into an upright position.

"Yeah," said Chase, scrolling through his phone. "All I could find was that we were flying into Ronald Reagan Washington National Airport, which used to be named Washington National."

"Well, I would have you all know that this airport also has a connection with an African American architect. His name was **Albert Irvin Cassell**, and he did some projects on this airport back when it was still called Washington National. He was the head of Howard's Architecture Department for a time as well. I'll tell you, kids, his work is pretty epic. He even has two of his projects on the U.S. National Registrar of Historic Places. His works can be found all over Washington, DC. From the time you touch down in the airport to the time you leave, you could very well be in sight of one of **Mr. Cassell's** projects or another. We'll see quite a bit of his legacy on Howard's campus once we tour there."

"I hope my brother knows all of this stuff!" Terrence said in amazement.

"I'm sure he does," his mother replied, joining in the conversation. "He is an architecture major after all. You should ask him about it."

"Cassell, I know that name," Akiya said from a few rows back.

"How can you hear the conversation all the way back there?" Marcus asked, craning his neck to see Akiya.

"Principal Davis said the information was for the STEAM Chasers, I had permission to hear. Anyway, Cassell, as in **Alberta Cassell**? She wrote the cutest little children's book called *The Little White Butterflies*, she even did the illustrations!"

"Nope, not the same person, we're talking about an architect, not a children's book author," said Chase, clearly proud that he could mark himself in the category of people who knew something Akiya didn't.

"Not so fast there, Chase," said Ebony. "Principal Davis wasn't talking about **Alberta Cassell**, but he could have been." She started to look for something in her backpack. They were now parked at the terminal and waiting to deplane.

"What are you looking for?" asked Shar who was looking over Ebony's shoulder.

"My tablet. I texted my mom and dad to let them know we landed, and I looked up Cassell after that."

"Just how fast are your fingers?" asked Marcus. "You type faster than Chase, and he's a hacker!"

Principal Davis gave Chase a glance.

"A White Hat hacker, that's an ethical hacker. I bring good to the universe, Principal Davis. You know me." Chase's smile was so big he was showing all of his teeth.

"Anyway," continued Ebony, "**Albert Cassell** is the architect Principal Davis was talking about. However, it says here he had eight kids. Four of them ended up going to Columbia University and three of them ended up being architects like their dad. **Alberta Cassell** was one of them! Well, she ended up becoming **Alberta Cassell Butler**. She was so amazing. Look at all this!"

Ebony handed her tablet to Shar. "Oh my gosh, she was like Wonder Woman. She worked for her dad's architecture firm; then she went on to become an architectural engineer for the Naval Research Laboratory. She even worked as an engineering draftswoman with the Military Sea Life Command and then went on to be a naval architect. The book Akiya was talking about, *The Little White Butterflies*, was actually published after she died. It says her daughter published it for her as a promise to her mom."

"What a sweet daughter," said Mrs. Worthington, who may very well have wiped a tear from her eye.

"So, is being an awesome architect genetic or something?" Chase seemed to be asking the question to no one as he grabbed his backpack from under his seat and started to stretch. People were now starting to file off the plane.

"No way. I hope I don't have to do what my dad does. He teaches all day. No offense, Principal Davis, but once I'm done with college, no way do I think I want to be back in school all day."

"No offense taken, Marcus. And, no, there is no reason for a kid to do what their parent does." Principal Davis gave Marcus a reassuring smile.

"I don't know, I wouldn't mind," said Terrence.

"Oh, have I convinced you to become an actuary?" asked his mom.

"Not quite yet, Mom. I was talking about Dad."

"I don't know, being an actuary sounds kind of fun. I might have that on my list," said Akiya as they walked off the plane and entered the terminal.

As they headed to baggage claim, the subject of careers was still swirling around them.

"I forgot; what's your dad's job called again?" asked Chase as Terrence found his bright purple bag moving along the silver carousel.

"Hmm, maybe I can explain it to you, young man," said a voice behind them.

Terrence turned around faster than he ever had in his life. "Dad! What are you doing here?" He ran and threw his arms around his dad.

"We just finished up our project, and I needed to debrief the captain. Come to find out, she had some business in DC she needed to take care of as well, so she said we could do the debriefing here in DC, and I get to take a few days off to hang out with you and your classmates."

"Terrence, dude, you are having a total family reunion right on our class trip." Chase gave Terrence a pat on the back.

"Now, Mr. Faulkner, tell us more about what you do. And do we call you Mr. or something else? I never quite know what to say to someone in uniform," Chase said admiringly.

Mr. Faulkner was kind enough to tell them about his latest mission as a member of the Army Corp of Engineers and how he joined the Corp as a part of the Army.

 Chapter 10

Terrence's head was spinning as he boarded the bus that was going to take them to the hotel. He was going to get a chance to hang out with his best friends, his brother, and his parents. Not bad at all.

"Alright, fellas, what's the plan?" Marcus whispered to Terrence and Chase.

They had only been on the bus a few minutes, and most of their classmates seemed to be trying to get in a quick nap.

"Plan for what?" asked Terrence.

"Revenge. Sweet, beautiful revenge."

"Oh yeah, we must be avenged for the wrong that was done to us," added Chase.

"Are you two talking about the girls? I think they got revenge on us. And it worked out. You have to admit we got to learn some cool information sitting with Principal Davis on that flight."

"That might be true, but we can't allow ourselves to be out-pranked. It's unnatural. The Lightning and Thunder being the best prankers in the world is natural. And, Terrence, this was your first big prank; you must come out on top." Chase gave Terrence a nudge.

"First of all, this was only my first big school prank, not my first prank. And second, I can admit when we've been bested."

"Oh, you've been holding back on us I see," said Marcus, sliding in closer to Terrence. "Spill it, my boy, who have you been pranking?"

"Just something I've been doing with my brother for years. You know, normal stuff. Certainly you two have pranked each other before."

"Nope," said Chase.

"Never," replied Marcus. "And you can only admit to being bested because you don't have the Lightning and Thunder reputation. We've got to work on that.

Hmm…" Marcus put his head back and started rubbing his chin.

"What?"

"Ah, yes. I see the problem," said Chase, not taking the same position as Marcus.

"What are you two talking about?"

"Terrence, there was something missing in our first collective prank. Do you know what it was?" Not waiting for Terrence to respond, Marcus continued, "Stealth. The stealth of a secret identity. Well, you know Lightning and Thunder speaks for itself. What, my friend, speaks for you?"

"I'm not really the secret identify type, guys. I just kind of let it all hang out."

"No way do you let it all hang out. If that were true, we would have known about your secret brother-pranking life. I'll tell you what, before we make it back home, you will have your identity!" Marcus gave Chase a victorious high five. "In the meantime, what do we do about the girls?"

"We have got to come up with a really good idea," said Chase.

Terrence looked over his shoulder at Shar. She caught him looking and tilted her head. She gave a mischievous smile then turned and started talking to Akiya and Ebony. Terrence had a feeling the girls were already on their way to developing their own plan as well.

As the bus pulled up to the hotel, Terrence got a text. It was from his brother. He and the other tour guides would be picking the class up at 8:00 in the morning. Terrence texted back that this was the same information on their agenda, so they were good to go. He showed the text to Chase and Marcus.

"That's it!" said Chase.

"What's it?" asked Terrence.

"You have the VIP tour connection. We'll tell the girls that your brother sent you a text saying the tour was going to start early. Let's give them a really early time, like six in the morning!"

"Wait, why do you keep using me and my brother as bait for the pranks?" Terrence didn't like where this was going. The girls might start thinking this was his idea.

"You're the glue that holds us all together, Terrence. Without you, there is no awesome. You help us all be awesome." The look on Chase's face made Terrence believe him.

"Glue I like; needing glue to put my ears back on my head after Shar rips them off for us making them wake up early—I don't like."

"I promise this will totally work." Marcus was already walking over to the girls.

Shar didn't believe the boys at first when they said Terrence's brother had changed the time of the tour.

"Why would you not believe it? This is going to be a VIP tour. It has to start early to see all of the amazing sights. You never know what we might be seeing on this trip," Chase said, clearly trying to sound believable.

"Well, you're going to be seeing stars if we don't really have to get up this early," said Shar.

"Without a telescope," added Ebony.

Terrence gulped.

He was relieved when Mrs. Worthington said everyone could head to their rooms and get settled in and they would be ordering pizza and having it delivered that night. Terrence didn't think he could face the girls any longer than he needed to.

He decided to text Trevor and tell him about the prank.

"Are you boys trying to die?" his brother texted back.

Terrence then wrote him about how the girls pranked them back.

His brother sent five smiling emojis and told him to accept defeat.

"Never," he typed in return. But he wasn't so sure about that never.

He then overheard Akiya talking to Shar. "Maybe the boys were being honest about the time being moved up. It sounds like Mrs. Worthington wants us in bed early since they are letting everyone go to their rooms now. The schedule said we should have had a briefing tonight from nine till ten. I guess that means bedtime is nine instead."

Terrence gulped again. This tour was going to need to be really good for the girls to forget about what they had set them up for—really good.

 Chapter 11

Terrence got dressed as slowly as he could. He wasn't looking forward to seeing just how mad Shar would be. He could pretty much tell from the four text messages he got from her that the girls had in fact gone downstairs to the lobby at 6:00 AM to wait for the tour bus. They had apparently waited fifteen minutes before they started to text the boys. They lasted until 6:30 when Shar texted they were going back to bed, but the boys better make sure they slept well because they wouldn't be getting a good night's sleep for a really long time.

"How bad do you think it will be?" asked Chase as he put on a black tie with green stripes.

"I think whatever the punishment is, it will be worth it!" said Marcus. "I can't imagine their faces when they realized no one else was coming. I think I can boldly say we are the undefeated winners of the prank war."

"You think so?" asked Terrence.

Just then, the phone rang in their hotel room. Chase picked it up slowly. "Hello?"

Marcus walked up behind Chase. "Is it Shar? How mad is she? Oh no, maybe it's Akiya, she is probably the most level-headed. I don't hear any screaming yet, so I vote Akiya."

Chase turned to Terrence. "Um, it's your mom." He handed Terrence the phone.

"Hey, Mom! We're on our way down." Terrence tried to sound calm.

"Oh yeah, you better be on your way down. And you better be on your way down with a very good excuse as to why Ebony, Akiya, and Shar got the idea that they needed to be down here at six in the morning."

"Yes, ma'am," was all Terrence could manage to get out of his mouth.

"Busted," whispered Chase.

"Big time," replied Marcus.

Terrence's cell phone started to buzz. He could see it was his brother calling. He started to talk as soon as Terrence said hello.

"Didn't I tell you to just take the L and keep it moving? I tried to warn you. You do realize boys rarely beat girls in the prank war. Not only are you going to get it from Mom, Shar is going to get you as well." His brother apparently found this extremely funny.

"Knock it off," replied Terrence. "Are you downstairs?"

"Yes, the other tour guides and I are downstairs. Now, get your hind parts down here so I can see what Mom does to you. She must be upset, she couldn't even remember your cell phone number, that's why she called the room. This is going to be good!"

***

Marcus was the first out of the elevator. Mrs. Faulkner was standing right outside the door.

"Hello, Mrs. Faulkner."

"Don't even try it, young man," said Terrence's mom.

"That bad?" asked Chase as he made his way off the elevator.

"That bad," said Mrs. Worthington who was standing next to Mrs. Faulkner.

"Mom, I can explain." Terrence had no idea what he was going to say next, but he didn't have to. His mom started talking.

"Oh, you don't have to explain to me. Ebony gave me all the details. Look, I was your age once, as was your dad. We understand you boys were just trying to have a little fun. However, there are rules of prank wars, and you know it."

"Yes, very important universal rules." Terrence's brother came up and put his arm around his mom and gave her a kiss on the cheek. "I tried to warn him, Mom."

"Oh, so you knew he was doing this and didn't tell me?" Mrs. Faulkner turned her attention to Trevor.

Trevor looked at Terrence and pointed his finger. "No way; this isn't on me. It's those guys. I tried to stop them, but I was overpowered." He started laughing as he backed away.

"Wait, I didn't hear about these prank rules. What rules?" asked Chase, looking to Terrence with a raised eyebrow.

"Prank rules mean you have to decide on the rules before the pranking starts. Since you boys didn't do that, we made a little concession for the girls. Shar, Ebony, and Akiya have asked that the three of you forgo punishment as long as they are allowed to exact their revenge however they choose. We agreed." Terrence's mom stepped back to show the girls standing behind her. The smile on Shar's face let Terrence know they were in for trouble. He dropped his head and walked toward the tour bus. This was going to be a long day after all.

Chase, Terrence, and Marcus found seats together on the bus, only to realize that Shar, Ebony, and Akiya were right behind them.

"Buckle up, boys, it is going to be quite the ride," said Ebony as she rubbed her hands together, smiling like the Cheshire Cat from *Alice in Wonderland*.

Luckily, they couldn't spend too much time worrying about what the girls might do to them. They were quickly pulling in to their first stop.

"Oh my gosh!" squealed Akiya. "The King Memorial!"

The bus pulled next to the curb, and everyone climbed out. Terrence looked up to see what appeared to be a huge chunk of granite.

"Where is the monument?" asked Marcus.

"On the other side—hurry!" Akiya led the way as Shar and Ebony took off behind her. Terrence had to run at full speed to catch up.

"Why isn't it done?" asked Chase. And in some ways, it did look like the sculpture wasn't finished. One of Dr. King's legs seemed to be stuck in the granite, and the back of his body wasn't carved out. What was there was huge. Even standing right next to the monument, Akiya didn't even reach Dr. King's knee, and she was the tallest kid in their group.

"It's supposed to look unfinished," said Mrs. Worthington gently. "Dr. King's work isn't yet done. I mean, we're closer than we were, but we're not there yet." Terrence hadn't even heard her and his mom come up next to them.

"Guess what, little brother," said Trevor. "Just a little something to put in the STEAM Chasers' book of amazing facts; the lead architect on this project was **Dr. Edward Jackson, Jr**. He was chosen by the president of the Alpha Phi Alpha Fraternity, Incorporated to lead the project. They were the ones who wanted a memorial. Dr. King was actually a member of Alpha Phi Alpha; he crossed through in nineteen fifty-two."

"What does cross through mean?" asked Ebony.

"It just means he became an official member of the fraternity. Do you all know it took thirteen years for legislation to get approved for the building of the memorial to start? **Dr. Jackson** was there every step of the way, making sure the Dr. King Memorial would live up to his legacy. I would say he did a great job."

"He sure did," said Principal Davis who was walking up to the group. "Make sure you all go around and read each of the inscriptions."

Terrence knew there were walls all around the memorial; he hadn't realized there was writing on all of them. Some people were already reading the words carved in stone that surrounded them. He could tell some people had been crying; he saw a number of people wiping their eyes and others hugging and touching the wall.

"This is absolutely amazing," said Shar as she walked arm and arm with Ebony and Akiya.

Terrence's brother gave him a wink. Maybe this tour would get the girls' minds off of their prank.

After about thirty minutes, another one of the tour guides told everyone it was time to get back on the bus and get ready for the next stop.

"I really wish I had brought one of my drones," said Marcus as he gave Dr. King's statue a pat goodbye. "I could have gotten some amazing pictures."

"That just means we have to come back some day and visit Dr. King again!" said Chase, giving his cousin an encouraging pat on the back.

***

The tour's next stop was the African American Civil War Memorial and Museum. The group walked silently past the pictures of brave looking soldiers dressed in uniforms.

Terrence heard his mother say, "You know, I don't think I ever learned about one Black soldier who fought in the Civil War."

"That's why it is so important to have these museums, Mom," Terrence heard his brother say.

"Oh my gosh, it's beautiful," Shar said loudly and rushed forward. She was heading toward what looked like a bronze statue.

"Great taste, Shar," said Trevor. "This is called *The Spirit of Freedom,* and the sculptor is **Dr. Ed Hamilton**."

"His work is incredible," said Ebony, circling the sculpture several times.

Akiya started taking pictures of the sculpture from every angle.

"Well, if you like this piece, you would really love his other works. He made a sculpture of Booker T. Washington that sits at Hampton University. He also has a huge sculpture that he did of Joe Louis that is located in Detroit, Michigan. One of my personal favorites is his Amistad Memorial that is located in New Haven, Connecticut."

"Amistad. I know that. It was the revolt that took place on the *La Amistad* ship that was trying to transport people into slavery, to force them to work on sugar plantations. They successfully revolted and were brought to Washington, DC by a naval ship. They won their freedom in court. It happened in eighteen thirty-nine."

"Akiya, I swear you are a walking encyclopedia," said Marcus.

"Well, I'm glad for it," Shar responded. "I had never heard of Amistad or a revolt or that people won their freedom."

"Well, they won the case eventually. It went all the way to the Supreme Court. But they won!"

"You are absolutely correct, Akiya," said Trevor. "They won. And **Dr. Hamilton** created a stunning memorial so that we would never forget their brave revolt against slavery and how they fought for freedom."

"Exactly why have I never heard about an amazing and successful revolt on a ship bound for slavery. Do you know how fun that would make history classes? They should be teaching about ship battles all the time!" Marcus looked at Principal Davis and shrugged his shoulders. "Sorry, I got a little carried away."

"No harm, Marcus. You're right; we can all stand to learn a bit more. If that battle intrigues you, I would encourage you to do some reading on **Robert Smalls** and how he managed to commandeer a heavily armed Confederate ship during the Civil War and take it all the way to the Union Amy."

"Are you writing that down, Terrence?" asked Chase. "Amistad and Robert Smalls."

"Why would I be writing it down?" asked Terrence.

"Don't worry, I'm writing it down," said Marcus, who was typing into the notes app on his phone.

"Oh, I was just expecting Akiya to remember it all," said Shar, and she gave her friend a squeeze.

"I wouldn't mind some official backup," said Akiya, smiling shyly.

 Chapter 12

The tour bus weaved its way around streets crowded with tourists, areas filled with government buildings, and residential areas with apartments and homes. Terrence could feel his classmates going into as much information overload as he was. He had no idea there were so many buildings that were designed or built by African Americans throughout the DC area.

This included the huge Mount Vernon Apartment Complex. One of the tour guides let the class know this apartment complex was designed by the Bryant Mitchell design firm and was featured as one of the outstanding living African American projects at the Chicago Athenaeum in 1993. The Bryant Mitchell firm was founded by **Charles Irving Bryant** and **Melvin L. Mitchell**, two amazing African American architects.

"Well, I know if they designed this building, they had to design a lot more. This building is mind-blowing," Chase said as he craned his neck out the window to get a better look.

"Right you are," said Trevor with a smile. "The firm also designed the Metro Center Mixed Use Development and the 'H' Street Center. They even designed the historic Dunbar High School. In fact, the firm designed over fifty educational facilities. The Dunbar High School project is three hundred forty thousand square feet!"

"Wow! You could fit at least ten Global Academies inside that school. And I thought our school was pretty big."

Terrence was always amazed at just how fast Ebony could calculate numbers. Her brain sometimes seemed like it functioned as its very own calculator.

Terrence's brother was back at the microphone and getting everyone's attention. "Okay, now we are going to make a very special stop that I am sure many of you will enjoy."

It seemed everyone started talking at once, trying to guess where they might be going next. Terrence couldn't think of a place. He knew they were going to the museum the next day, so that wouldn't be it. They drove for about twenty minutes, and the bus stopped in a very unexpected spot.

"Did we break down?" asked Chase.

"Maybe it's a bathroom break," Marcus suggested, trying to position himself so that he could see out the window.

"Alright, folks, what do you think?" Trevor asked the clearly confused bus of students and chaperones.

"I thought we were going to see another building that was designed by an African American architect," said Akiya.

"We are," said Trevor, smiling. "Right outside."

"But this isn't really a building, it's a stadium," said Ebony, a bit confused.

"Not just any field, Ebony," said Trevor. "This is Audi Field, home of D.C. United Soccer team!"

"No way!" shouted someone in the back.

"I love DC United!" screamed another.

"I'm glad you all are so excited. The associate architect for this stadium was none other than **Michael Marshall**. He owns the Michael Marshall Design firm, and this stadium is just one of their signature projects. The stadium is close to five hundred thousand square feet and can hold twenty thousand fans. Well, what are you all waiting for? Grab your stuff. We get to look inside!"

Everyone started cheering and grabbing their things to pile out of the tour bus. They were greeted by three stadium employees who were waiting at the door with lanyards for each of them as well as a DC United bag filled with hats, towels, key chains, and even mini soccer balls.

"Right this way," said one of the hosts who was standing inside the door. "We have some wonderful things planned for you all this afternoon."

"Like what?" asked Chase as he was pulling his soccer ball out of his bag.

"Like giving you all a tour of a few of our luxury suites, letting you all get a feel for what it is like sitting in the front row. We might even have permission for you all to get a quick run across the field."

"I knew I should have brought my drone!" said Marcus, slapping himself on the top of his head.

"I know that has to be disappointing," said the host. "Maybe we can do something to make up for that. Each of you is also getting a twenty-five-dollar gift card to use in the gift shop."

"Oh, that makes me feel a little better," said Marcus with a huge grin.

"Well, I guess I didn't even need to tell you about the catered lunch you all were having," said the host, now laughing herself.

"Now that you mention it, I am hungry!" said Chase. "Hopefully we are eating first."

Trevor came up and gave Chase a fun tap on the shoulder. "You know it. Lunch is waiting; then we get the full tour and some time on the field."

"This tour is going to be awesome!" Shar was jumping up and down and taking pictures of everything she passed.

Trevor gave Terrence a smile.

"Good work, brother. Good work," Terrence mouthed to his brother.

After the group finished their lunch, they started a tour of the stadium. They got to see every piece of the massive building and then it was time for what everyone was waiting for, getting a chance to go onto the field. The hosts even grabbed some soccer balls to let the group have the ultimate experience.

Shar, Ebony, and Akiya were talking with Terrence, Chase, and Marcus as they all walked to the field. One of their hosts walked up to them with a new person they hadn't seen during the tour.

"Hey! I'm an engineer who works here at the stadium. I was wondering if anyone was interested in pyrotechnics." The woman was beaming as she spoke.

"Rockets!" screamed Ebony.

"Chemicals!" shouted Shar.

"Hey, you two, are you crazy? We are in the nation's capital; you can't be talking about chemical rockets! The secret service could show up and arrest us all!" Marcus was shaking his head.

"No, silly," said Ebony. "Pyrotechnics is the technical name for fireworks that you see during sporting events and holidays. They are shot up with rockets, and the colors come from the use of chemicals."

"Absolutely," said the engineer. "I guess I have found my volunteers. Ladies, follow me!" She led them down a hall, followed closely by Mrs. Worthington.

"Want to come, Akiya?" Shar called back toward Akiya.

"No, I'm good. I'm about to go score a goal on Chase."

"I'll take that bet," said Marcus.

"Oh, I'll do you one better, I'll let you in the goal with him."

"Nope, too easy. I have an idea. Chase and I will play defense, and we'll let Terrence play goalie. If you manage to get it past the both of us and score, I'll eat my hat."

"Oh, I'm definitely taking these odds." Akiya smiled.

Terrence wanted to object, but everyone was already walking toward the field. He thought Marcus must have forgotten that he wasn't the best in soccer, or football, or most other sports that involved a ball.

It took less than five minutes for Akiya to score.

"Terrence, what were you doing? You're supposed to be our last line of defense," shouted Marcus.

"Um… you aren't supposed to need your last line of defense. In fact, if you are relying on the last line of defense, something horrible happened much earlier and it couldn't have been my fault."

"We were just warming up, Akiya. Let's go again," shouted Chase.

Terrence knew Chase would keep asking for another shot until they managed to block a goal. He was a great athlete. However, Akiya was fast, very fast. And she was always trying to inject some sort of physics into her moves. She seemed to always be able to predict where the ball was going. "Physics, boys, physics," she kept saying with each shot.

About thirty minutes later, Terrence saw Shar and Ebony helping the engineer roll a large cart on to the edge of the field and start to set up something that looked like large pipes. He probably should have been looking at the goal, but he was intrigued. He looked down just in time to see the ball roll past him again and into the goal. He was sure Marcus was about to say something, but over the loudspeaker, he heard someone say, "Okay, everyone, we have a surprise for you. Count down with me. Five... four... three... two... one..."

As everyone reached the number one, bright red fireworks shot up into the air above the stadium. Kids shouted and cheered as they clapped for the show.

Before long, it was time to head back to the bus. Terrence noticed Shar, Akiya, and Ebony running in front of them.

"What's their hurry?" asked Chase.

"Akiya's probably telling them how she scored on us three times in a row. Three times!" Marcus had clearly been taking score.

By the time the three boys had boarded the bus, the girls were already sitting down. There was an empty seat in front of them.

"Mind if we join you three?" asked Chase, smiling.

"Oh, we were counting on it." Shar smirked.

They would soon find out why the three girls were counting on it. It all happened so fast. They sat down in unison; then came the sound, next the smell, and finally the feeling. Terrence was the first to jump up.

"What in the world?"

Marcus was fast behind him. "Please tell me there's nothing on the back of my pants!"

Chase was trying to swipe at his backside and hold his nose at the same time.

People started roaring with laughter. Terrence looked down at his seat.

"A whoopie cushion?"

Marcus picked up a plastic bag that looked like it had gel on the inside. "And what exactly is this?"

"What is that smell? Open a window!" shouted Chase as he waved at Terrence.

"Like what we found in the gift shop, boys?" Akiya was laughing so hard she could hardly get the words out.

The girls had run ahead to set up their prank. Terrence had to admit it worked flawlessly.

Once Marcus and Chase came back to their senses, they burst into laughter.

"Okay, that was classic," said Chase, giving Ebony a high five.

"Proof!" said Marcus triumphantly.

"Proof of what?" asked Akiya.

"Proof that a puppy army whose primary weapon was smart smell would work as a weapon of battle.

Thanks so much, my ladies, for running our first ever field test."

Now Terrence had joined in with the laughter as well.

"Wait, the puppy army you all talked about at the presentation was real?" asked Principal Davis.

"It's a long story," said Terrence.

"Oh, I think the ride back to the hotel will be enough time for me to hear it."

***

On the way back, Marcus and Chase pitched their puppy army concept; the rest of the kids congratulated Shar, Ebony, and Akiya as being the first kids in the school to publicly prank the best prankers in history, and everyone had a great time.

Terrence was actually relieved. He no longer had to wait to see what the girls were going to do to them for their early morning prank. They had gotten their revenge, and it was pretty fun. Akiya even said he could keep the whoopie cushion. Of course, he couldn't use it on his brother, who was one of the tour guides on the bus, but he did wonder what his dog might do if he sat down on the cushion. He seemed to be filled with real farts most of the time anyway.

***

When they got to the hotel, Terrence's dad was waiting for them.

"Well, famous STEAM Chasers, I got permission from Principal Davis and text confirmations from all of your parents that I could take you all to dinner. Plus, I get to officially join your school group on your tour of the museum tomorrow."

Terrence was so happy, he thought he would burst. On the way to the restaurant, they told Mr. Faulkner about all of the things they learned.

"I am amazed. The only person I learned much about in school was **Benjamin Banneker**."

"The clock guy?" asked Terrence.

"Yes, he was famous for building his own wooden clock from scratch. He also worked as a surveyor for the land that would become our nation's capital."

"What's a surveyor?" asked Shar.

"Well, one of the things they do is measure land to make precise property boundaries. They establish boundaries for land, airspace, and even water boundaries. They determine who owns what as well as where buildings and other built spaces can go. You can't do any major building in this country without first getting the land surveyor to ensure you own the property lines and won't encroach on anyone else's lines. Since Washington, DC was going to be the place for the nation's brand-new capital, the survey had to be perfect. They wanted to make sure no state got more pieces of the pie than they should."

"Didn't **Benjamin Banneker** also have an almanac?" asked Ebony.

"Right you are," said Mr. Faulkner. "**Benjamin Banneker** is what we would call a renaissance individual. That's a person who is really good at a lot of things, and for **Mr. Banneker**, many of those things were self-taught—astronomy, woodworking, mechanics. He was even an activist. He wrote to Thomas Jefferson and said that he hoped Jefferson would embrace every opportunity to eradicate the train of the absurd and false ideas and opinions about Black people. To prove Black people were just as smart as anyone else, he included a handwritten copy of his almanac for seventeen ninety-two, which included many astronomical calculations as proof of the genius that Black people held."

"Seventeen ninety-two, my goodness," said Mrs. Faulkner. "And to think, slavery still wasn't abolished until eighteen sixty-five."

"Why didn't Jefferson listen? And why don't we learn about things like his almanac and **Michael Marshall** and the stadium as all the other amazing things African Americans have done?"

"That's a good question," said Mrs. Faulkner, giving Terrence a pat on the hand.

"Well, that's why the world needs the STEAM Chasers," said Marcus.

"Yeah, you're right." Terrence sighed. "But I think the world might need more than that as well." He sat back in his seat and let his head rest on the window. His mind began to wonder about what the world needed to remember the contributions of so many African Americans.

 Chapter 13

"I got it!" After sitting at the desk in their hotel room for over an hour, Terrence finally had what he was looking for.

"Got what? It's like four in the morning." Marcus yawned.

"It's not four, it's six thirty," said Terrence.

"Is that supposed to be better? Because in my world, those are pretty much the same time," said Chase, poking his head from under the covers. "What are you doing up at this time anyway?"

Terrence got up and stretched. "Working. I couldn't sleep because I was trying to figure something out."

"What code are you cracking now?" asked Chase.

The two cousins knew Terrence all too well. When he had something on his mind, he could be relentless in pursuing it. After all, that was how he found out their secret identities with the comic they used to write.

"The detective is at it again," said Marcus, still talking through yawns.

"That's it! How could I not have thought of that before?" Chase was now springing up from his bed.

"Okay, now you both have me confused, so I'm going back to sleep."

"No! We've been promising my man Terrence his identity for so long, and it was right in front of us. See, I had missed it because I thought it would be weather related, like ours. I mean we are Thunder and Lightning."

"No, that would be Lightning and Thunder," Marcus interrupted.

Chase walked over to his bed, grabbed a pillow, and threw it at Marcus. "I'll give you that one only because lightning actually comes first in nature. But we both know who was the fastest on that soccer field yesterday."

Terrence couldn't help but chime in, "Yeah, Akiya." He was glad Chase was out of pillows to throw.

"Anyway, because we were thinking weather, nothing was quite sticking. Hurricane, tornado, rainstorm, sunshine, none of it fit."

"Please don't tell me you thought for one minute to call me sunshine."

Marcus started laughing. "Oh, those are only the names we care to admit to out loud. We went to some interesting naming places when we ventured into the animal kingdom. How do you feel about antelopes and butterflies?"

"I feel like I'm really glad you all couldn't find a name that you thought fit me. Now I don't know whether to be excited or scared about what Chase says next."

"No fears, it's great, and it's you. Without further ado, I give you your new persona—the Detective!"

Marcus was now jumping out of his bed. "Yes! That is perfect! You are like a determined badger when there is something you need to hunt down. You can be slick and sly, which is how you figured us out. And you always fake being quiet so people talk a lot around you."

"Um … I'm not faking being quiet, I actually am quiet," Terrence protested.

"No, we thought you were quiet. We've been watching you since we've been here in DC. You're real comfortable talking with college students and military people and other adults."

"Well, one of those college students is my brother, the military person is my dad, and my mom is on the trip as one of the chaperones. She and Mrs. Worthington are good friends, so I'm around her even outside of school every once in a while."

"Brutal. I mean Mrs. Worthington is the best teacher in the world, but that doesn't mean I want to see my teachers outside of school very often. She'd know I waited until the last minute to do my homework."

"I think we all know you wait until the last minute to do your homework, Marcus, especially when you ask Mrs. Worthington how many words an essay was supposed to be while we're in class about to turn it in." Chase laughed.

"That was one time!"

"She isn't over to my house all the time or anything like that. I don't hate the Detective, especially since I know the alternatives. I'll try it on for the day. But first, can I tell you two what I came up with this morning?"

"Sure," said Chase and Marcus in unison.

"The Blackprint!"

"The what now?" asked Chase with a raised eyebrow.

"The Blackprint," Terrence answered with a smile.

"And what is this Blackprint?" asked Chase.

"Wait, before you answer that, let me call the girls' room. They probably want to hear this, too. Right?" said Marcus.

***

Shar, Ebony, and Akiya agreed to meet downstairs in the lobby so Terrence could go over his idea with them before the shuttle picked them up to go to the museum. They would grab their breakfast and a table in the corner.

"Okay, Terrence. Let's hear this great idea," said Shar, putting down her tray of oatmeal and fruit.

Terrence took a deep breath before he started speaking. He didn't know why he always got nervous when he was going to present one of his own ideas, even when speaking to his friends. But he had worked hard on this, and he really did think it was great. At least it felt like something they could do to make things right. So, he exhaled and started to share his plan for the Blackprint.

"Okay, I was thinking about how much we have been learning about the contributions that African Americans have made all through Washington, DC. But if no one was there to tell us, we wouldn't have known it. And then I thought about what happened with Marie Van Brittan Brown and how we can't even figure out what she looked like. It felt like they were being lost to time, even the people who are still alive and well today. I wanted us to be able to do something about it. So then, it hit me—the Blackprint!"

"That's what we're trying to figure out, Detective, what's the Blackprint?" asked Marcus.

"Detective?" asked Ebony, tilting her head.

"It's a long story, we'll tell you on the bus," said Chase.

"The Blackprint," Terrence continued, "is sort of like a cross between a blueprint and a fingerprint. So, what's a fingerprint?"

"A fingerprint is the impression that's left after you touch something with your finger. They can even identify people by the fingerprint they leave because everyone is unique," answered Akiya.

"Perfect. Now, what's a blueprint?"

"Oh, I know this one!" said Marcus. "It's a technical drawing, like the official plans for a building, or really anything. It shows you what the designer intended for whatever they were creating."

"Exactly!" exclaimed Terrence. "So, that is what we have to do. We have to figure out a way to get the equivalent of a fingerprint or blueprint onto the things that African Americans have designed. That way, when you walk into Audi Field, there is a way to know the designer was **Michael Marshall**."

"Oh!" said Shar. "Or when you go to look up **Marie Van Brittan Brown**, you know you are seeing a picture of her and not **Bessie Blount Griffin**."

"Yes!" Terrence was so excited he nearly jumped out of his chair. But he always knew his friends would get it, they were the STEAM Chasers after all.

"So, how do we get the Blackprint thing going?" asked Terrence.

"Well, that is the part that I haven't figured out yet," Terrence replied.

"No worries," said Marcus. "Sherlock Holmes was known for solving the crime not necessarily building robots."

"Plus, we're a team. I'm sure the six of us can come up with some ideas," said Chase.

They spent the next fifteen minutes finishing off breakfast and brainstorming. They then saw it was time to head for the bus that was taking them to the National Museum of African American History and Culture. It was going to be a very interesting journey!

***

The bus ride went quickly, as it was filled with excitement from all the students. Terrence could hear Ryan telling Abigail and Tyrone that he had been to the museum once before on a trip with his family. He saw Rebecca sketching feverishly as if she was trying to catch the ever-changing landscape. Asher and Charlotte were discussing what they might try to find in the gift shop. Darren and Keisha were playing rock-paper-scissors while Zion and Avery were trying to launch Beyblades on their cramped seat. At the same time, Chase, Marcus, Shar, Ebony, and Akiya were all trying to figure out how to create a tangible Blackprint. Terrence would have contributed to the conversation, but his brain felt fried from coming up with the idea in the first place. So he just sat back and people watched for the moment.

Before long, the bus was pulling up to a huge building that resembled an upside-down pyramid growing right from the ground. The perfectly manicured green lawn was inviting as everyone piled off the bus. Terrence turned to see his father walking with his mother toward the group.

"Hi, Dad!" said Terrence; he always thought his father looked so official when he was in his military uniform. "You official today?"

"Absolutely," answered his dad. "I get the honor to tour with you all and point out some things the Army

Corps of Engineers have been involved with as we go through the museum."

"Let's get this party started," said Marcus as he headed toward the entrance.

Chase entered the museum and went straight to the Welcome Desk that greeted visitors from the Mall entrance. "Hi, I would like to report a crime."

Akiya looked as if she might faint. Shar's mouth fell open. Ebony raised her eyebrows so high they almost touched her bangs. Terrence had no idea what Chase was talking about.

"Was this part of a plan that you all forgot to tell us?" Shar asked Marcus.

"I have no clue," said Marcus.

The round-faced woman in rimmed glasses who was working the front desk had no idea what Chase was talking about either it seemed. "Young man, if you have witnessed a crime, you probably need to contact the police. Is he with you, sir? Can you help him?" the woman said as she looked toward Mr. Faulkner.

"No, not that sort of crime," replied Chase. "I am here to report a Blackprint crime. More specifically, a case of identity swapping that is severely interfering with the appropriate identification of one of America's best inventors, as well as her equally amazing counterpart, who is also a victim I might add."

A very official looking woman stepped up beside the greeter and looked inquisitively at Chase. "A Blackprint crime, can you tell me what that is?"

"Well, I'll let my friend Terrence tell you all about the Blackprint!" Chase then patted Terrence on the back and walked him closer to the desk.

Terrence felt his heart start racing and gulped hard. His dad came up close behind him. "Go ahead, Terrence, I'm interested in hearing what the Blackprint is as well."

Terrence then laid out the same description of the Blackprint he had laid out to his friends earlier.

"That is amazing!" said the mystery woman. "I love the concept of the Blackprint. Now, tell me about this Blackprint crime."

"Oh, that's all, Chase," Terrence said quickly and stepped back behind his dad.

Chase cleared his throat. "So, you heard what the Blackprint is; now I get to tell you about why it is so important. We were doing some research on Bessie Blount Griffin, mainly because her work in forensics foiled the best prank ever, but that's another story. Anyway, I come across a picture of her and, what do you know, it's the same picture as **Marie Van Brittan Brown**! I know that can't be right because they weren't sisters or anything like that. But really official looking websites are using the exact same picture as if they were the same person. It's a crime!"

The woman walked around the desk and stood in front of Chase. "You're right, and that is why this museum is so important. And we reach out whenever we see that problem happening. I'm Dr. Wexler, one of the curators of this museum." She reached out to shake everyone's hand.

"What happens when you reach out to people and tell them?" asked Akiya.

"Well, some websites have taken down the erroneous picture," answered Dr. Wexler.

"That doesn't seem quite right," said Shar gently. "I mean having the wrong picture is bad, but the correction shouldn't be just to make Marie Van Brittan Brown faceless."

"You're right," answered the curator. "We're still trying to figure out a better fix."

"Sounds like you need trained assassins," said Marcus.

"What?" asked Mr. Faulkner.

"Oh, not *those* kinds of assassins," Marcus responded.

"Are there other types of assassins?" asked Mr. Faulkner, shifting a bit on his feet.

"I don't think he means assassins," Ebony said from the back of their small group. "Marcus, are you talking about coding ninjas that Chase told us about before?"

"Oh yeah, assassins, ninjas—is there a big difference?" he asked, apparently surprised by the faces staring at him.

"A big difference," said Mr. Faulkner, letting out a huge sigh.

"Yeah, maybe you could get some really good coders who could write software that would automatically correct bad information," Chase interjected excitedly.

"Now, that sounds like a good idea. We'll have to think about that as one of our considerations. Thank you for sharing." Dr. Wexler gave Chase a big smile. "However, leave the crime part for us to deal with; I want you all to have as much time today in the museum as possible. You will be going through the exhibits, then having lunch in the Sweet Home Café, and we have a special presentation for your class just outside of our interactive gallery."

"What's the presentation on?" asked Akiya.

"African American women in architecture." The words seemed to sing from Dr. Wexler's mouth.

"Principal Davis said you all were learning quite a bit about architects and designers, so we created a special presentation just for your group that we think will be pretty fun."

"I can't wait!" shouted Shar.

"Well, let's get this tour started," said Mr. Faulkner.

"I have been waiting so long for this moment," said Mrs. Faulkner.

With that, the group headed toward the elevator to begin their museum experience.

 Chapter 14

Terrence couldn't even figure out how to take in all of the sights and sounds that surrounded him. Around every corner of the museum was something new and unexpected. He looked over to see Ebony pulling out an extra battery charger for her tablet. She had been taking so many notes, her battery had already died twice. Akiya was on her third notebook. Shar was taking pictures, while Chase and Marcus were trying to note down all of the crimes they saw, which meant things they felt they should have already known about African American history but hadn't been exposed to yet.

"The Blackprint is going to be huge, Detective, huge!" shouted Marcus.

Terrence approached where Marcus and Chase were standing in front of a display for someone named **George Washington Carver**.

"Terrence, this is your kind of dude. He was into the environment too!" Chase was guiding Terrence closer to the display. "He had his own laboratory at a college and everything."

"See, he was a detective, like you, Detective," added Marcus.

Akiya walked up behind Terrence. "Hey, look, he has three patents as well."

"Well, I'm impressed that he came up with a hundred and five recipes for the peanut. Of course, my family can't eat peanuts because my little brother is allergic, but I can respect the effort," Shar said, reading over the display.

"No worries," said Ebony. "It says he also came up with a lot of ways to use sweet potatoes. In fact, a ton of ways. This says he created seventy-three dyes, seventeen wood fillers, fourteen different types of candy, five types of paste, five breakfast foods, and even three different types of molasses."

"All that from the sweet potato?" asked Shar excitedly.

"The man was clearly a genius," said Akiya.

"See, I told you the Blackprint was going to be huge. His picture should be on every sweet potato sold in stores!" said Marcus.

"That might be a bit much and beyond what I was thinking about the Blackprint," said Terrence.

Mr. Faulkner was now standing at the display with the others. "Did you all know even this building is part of the Blackprint? I think it is, if I understand the Blackprint correctly."

"How so?" asked Terrence.

"Well, the architect who led the design for this building was the legendary **Philip Goodwin Freelon**. But most people called him **Phil Freelon**. I actually had an opportunity to meet him once when the Army Corp of Engineers was working on a project and I needed a bit of advice. The man was astonishing. Plus, he was married to the incredibly talented jazz singer and composer **Nenna Freelon**."

"I've heard of her!" shouted Ebony, excited. "My mom listens to her, especially her album *Homefree*."

"An architect and a jazz singer, no wonder this building is so awesome. Every corner of this building feels like an inspirational song singing its own tune and carrying you away in history," said Mrs. Faulkner.

"And that, Mom, is what the Blackprint is all about!" said Terrence, swaying next to his mom as if he were hearing a tune from one of Nenna Freelon's albums right in that moment.

"Well, I hate to break up the groove, you two," said Mr. Faulkner, "but my watch and my stomach say it might be time for lunch."

***

They made their way to the Sweet Home Café. Terrence couldn't believe all of the delicious sounding choices on the menu. He settled on a bowl of gumbo but also managed to taste some of his mom's shrimp and grits and the platter of greens and okra his dad had ordered. Terrence looked around, and everyone seemed to be enjoying every aspect of their lunch. Chase and Marcus even hatched a plan to buy their parents the cookbook the café sold.

"We figure we could get them to have a cooking competition using recipes from the book. They love challenging each other to cook-offs. So, if we keep the competition going, we just might convince them to cook everything in this book!" Chase and Marcus gave each other a high five.

"Just make sure you invite me over when the cook-off happens," said Terrence.

Shar looked up and said, "And me!"

Then Akiya, "And me!"

Ebony chimed in between bites of cornbread, "And me!"

"And don't forget me!" said Principal Davis, putting away his own copy of the cookbook that he purchased. "But in the meantime, everyone, I think it's time for us to head to the classroom for our presentation."

***

It took the groups of students around fifteen minutes to empty their trays and make their way to the classroom. The STEAM Chasers decided to sit together and got seats as close to the front as they could.

Ebony found a nearby outlet and plugged in her tablet. "I have a feeling I'm going to be doing a lot of writing during this presentation. I want to be ready!"

They looked up to see Dr. Wexler coming into the classroom. She flashed them a smile and got everyone's attention. She introduced the speaker and, just as she was heading toward her seat, she pointed to the group sitting eagerly toward the front, pens and tablets ready to go.

The speaker began. "Well, it seems I have a pretty big mandate. I hope to do you all proud, but if I leave anything out or if you want more information, feel free to stop me anytime to ask questions."

The speaker began by dimming the lights and turning on a projector. She typed a few things on her laptop then grabbed a laser pointer. The first picture to come onto the screen was a huge building. It looked like it was a half U shape with a large monument in front. The building looked very official, but Terrence couldn't place it.

"Does anyone know what this picture is?"

Even though it was dark, Terrence could tell everyone in class had turned toward where Akiya was sitting.

He heard her voice from the darkened room; she was sitting almost next to him. "I'm not sure the name of the building, but I think it's in France."

"Very good, this building is in France, and it is a very important building. It is the UNESCO United Nations Headquarters in Paris. Now, why do you all think I am showing you a picture of a building in Paris,

France at the National Museum of African American History and Culture?

"Because an African American designed the building?" Terrence heard Shar's voice rise from the darkness.

"Absolutely," said the speaker. "And not just any African American but architect **Beverly Loraine Greene**. She was the first Black woman licensed to be an architect in the United States. She was also the first African American woman to earn a degree in architectural engineering from the University of Illinois."

"Wait, you can be an architect and an engineer?" said a voice from further back in the room. Terrence recognized it as his classmate, Maya Lin. He remembered hearing her tell some other girls in the class that she was named after a famous Chinese American architect who designed the Vietnam Veterans Memorial.

"Absolutely!" exclaimed the speaker. "Architectural engineering is very popular, particularly for those who love math, design, and science."

"Now I want to be that too," said another student in the class Terrence recognized as Rebekah.

The speaker gave a warm smile through the glow of the projector and continued with the presentation. "**Beverly Loraine Greene** didn't just design buildings in France; she also designed buildings here in the United States, many on college campuses like the University of Arkansas and Sarah Lawrence College."

She used her pointer and flipped to the next picture. This one was an epic design of glass and color, bright red, blue, and green. It looked like something from the future. "This is the Pacific Design Center located in West Hollywood, California. The designer was **Norma Merrick Sklarek**. She was the first Black woman to become a licensed architect in both New York and California. In addition to this sleek and modern building, she also led the design for the Mall of

America and the embassy of the United States in Tokyo, Japan."

The next group of pictures showed pictures of the National Museum of African American History and Culture.

"Hey, I thought that was **Philip Goodwin Freelon**," said Ebony, a little confused after hearing Mr. Faulkner speak earlier.

"True, **Mr. Freelon** was one of the lead architects in the design of this building. However, there are usually quite a few people and organizations that work together to bring a project to life. One of the companies that ensured this museum came into being was McKissack and McKissack. The president of the firm is **Deryl McKissack**. In addition to this project, her firm worked on a number of amazing projects," answered the speaker. She flipped through photos and told the students about places such as the Navy Pier Centennial Projects in Chicago, Illinois, the Honda Aircraft Facilities in Greensboro, North Carolina, and even the McMillan Reservoir Stormwater Storage Facility right there in Washington, DC.

"Wow!" said Chase excitedly. "That looks like a cave."

Marcus started rubbing his hands together. "I could make my drone do some fantastic flying in that place."

A picture of the DC United Soccer Stadium was the next picture on the screen.

"We were there just yesterday," said Shar.

"McKissack and McKissack worked on the infrastructure of the stadium. So, it was built with good hands," said the speaker.

The next picture was of a woman who looked just like the one they had seen in pictures from McKissack and McKissack. The speaker turned back to the students and asked, "So, does anyone know who this is?"

Terrence raised his hand. The speaker saw him through the glare of light from the projector and motioned to him to answer. "You just told us, right? It's **Deryl McKissack**."

"Good guess, but nope, that isn't her."

Chase bolted upright in his seat. "Oh, man, another Blackprint crime. Because there is no way that isn't the same person we just saw. Well, unless she has a twin."

The speaker smiled. "That's right. This is **Cheryl McKissack** Daniel, twin sister of **Deryl McKissack**. **Cheryl's** work is just as impressive. Take a look at some of her projects." As the speaker flipped through the pictures, Terrence couldn't believe his eyes. **Cheryl's** company had done work on JFK International Airport, LaGuardia Airport, and Philadelphia International Airport. Her company had also done work with Pier 57, called "SuperPier," Billie Jean King National Tennis Center, and Lincoln Financial Field. They had even worked on hospitals, including the Harlem Hospital Center and the Perelman Center for Advanced Development. Almost everything one could think of from schools to train stations had crossed the path of **Cheryl McKissack Daniel** and her company.

The speaker continued, "What makes **Cheryl McKissack Daniel's** feat so amazing is that she is running the New York office of the oldest minority and women-owned professional design and construction firm in the nation. In fact, she is the fifth generation of the McKissack family to run the firm."

"Five generations!" said Akiya. "How old is the company?"

"The family-owned company has been around for more than a hundred and fifteen years, and they have helped to bring to completion more than six thousand projects."

"They've been in business since the early nineteen hundreds," said Ebony.

The group saw even more pictures of projects and were more impressed by the minute. In what seemed like much too short of a time, the presentation was over, and everyone began to file slowly out of the classroom.

"That was so cool," said Marcus.

"I feel bad," said Akiya.

"What?" asked Terrence. He would have thought the presentation would have made her excited, not sad.

"Well, I had never considered women architects before. I am ashamed to say I never looked at a building or airport or sports stadium and thought maybe a woman designed it or was the lead person in charge of the construction."

Terrence understood. "Don't worry, Akiya. That's why we need the Blackprint. If you weren't thinking about African American women designing and building hospitals or piers, I'm sure not many other people were. But we're going to do something about it. We're going to change that."

"Exactly," said Marcus. "And, really, don't feel bad. People are still surprised when I tell them what Chase's mom does. They think she is a real estate agent—they usually have no idea she actually is a home remodeler. Well, at least until she shows up on site with a construction helmet and sledgehammer."

"I have to admit, my mom does look pretty intimidating with that hammer."

173

"It's funny," began Shar, "Cheryl and Deryl are twins, and they both went into civil engineering and construction, but your moms are twins, and they didn't go into the same thing."

"Not at all," said Marcus. "My mom hates dust. But they both do things related to math and science, just in different ways."

"That's true," answered Shar.

The group did a bit more touring, and Mr. Faulkner stopped often to talk to students in the class about various exhibits, particularly the military ones. Before long, it was time to head back to the hotel. Everyone was disappointed they had to leave, there was so much more to see.

"We are going to have to plan a trip back," Mrs. Faulkner told Terrence. "No way could we see everything in one day. We might need a week to cover each nook and cranny."

"That would be fine with me!" Terrence smiled.

 Chapter 15

Terrence woke up to the sun shining in his face and his phone going off. It was a text from his brother telling him that he owed him big time.

"You owe him for what?" asked Marcus who was peering over Terrence's shoulder as he checked his phone again once he got out of bed.

"I have no idea. We're going to his campus today, and I think he is playing tour guide again."

"Well," began Chase, "you have to admit he hooked us up in the most epic way with that trip to the soccer stadium. I'm not sure he can top that."

The boys dressed quickly and headed downstairs to breakfast. Shar, Ebony, and Akiya were already downstairs.

"What took you guys so long?" asked Shar.

"What? We're not late," Chase griped.

"We want to make sure we get good seats on the bus. Despite you boys' terrible prank, we are still looking forward to visiting Howard's campus." Shar was putting her backpack on as she walked toward the door.

"At least let us get some food," said Marcus.

"Grab something to go, the bus is here." Ebony let the words fly behind her as she walked quickly to catch up with Akiya, whose long stride meant she was at the door before anyone else.

The boys grabbed some muffins and apples and followed after Ebony and Shar. The bus was ready with the door open by the time they got there.

"I am so excited." Ebony was almost shaking as she talked. "Did you know that Howard University was founded in eighteen sixty-seven, just two years after slavery was abolished?"

"So many amazing people graduated from Howard," Akiya added. "**Thurgood Marshall**, the first African American Supreme Court Justice,

Congressman and Civil Rights activist **Elija Cummings**, even Former Virginia **Governor Douglas Wilder**—he was the first African American governor in the country."

"That's all fine and good, but you left off some equally important people," said Chase, "**Chadwick Boseman**, the Black Panther himself, and **Ta-Nehisi Coates**, who wrote some current issues of the *Black Panther* comic book series."

"What about the ladies?" said Shar. "Writer **Zora Neale Hurston**, **Toni Morrison**, and **Patricia Roberts Harris**—she worked as a diplomat!"

"Well, it sounds like you all have done some homework," said Principal Davis, smiling as he passed the group.

***

Before long, the bus was off and headed to Howard University. In what seemed like no time, they were piling off the bus and going through an iron gate. Trevor met them right inside the gate. "Hey! How is my favorite school class in the world? Did you all miss me?"

Terrence heard a couple of girls giggle at those words. "Well, first, I'm going to take you all to the quad. You can get a feel for the enormity of the campus from there."

Terrence was impressed with just how much his brother knew about the campus. Akiya squealed with delight when Trevor said the first building they would go into was Founders Library.

"Be careful, Akiya," teased Marcus, "remember, you can't take anything since you don't have a library card."

"Akiya going into a library and not leaving with a book? Impossible." Chase laughed.

"Don't worry, Akiya. I'll make sure we get to the bookstore. They have a ton of great books you can leave with," said Trevor.

Akiya stuck out her tongue at Marcus and Chase and bounded into the library.

Shar fell in love with the chemistry building, and she beamed as if she was already a student when she learned it was the chemistry department that awarded the first PhD from the university.

Ebony had to be pried away from the department of physics and astronomy. Terrence thought she just might faint as Trevor told her about how students in astronomy classes used the Locke Hall Observatory telescope. However, Ebony had company when they went to the mechanical engineering department and learned about the aerospace engineering program. Marcus was happy that designing and building things to fly was a legitimate college major.

Chase couldn't decide if he liked computer science or computer engineering better as they explored the various computing facilities, including the Howard Nanoscale Science and Engineering Facility.

Terrence was just trying to take it all in, although his brother nudged him a lot when they got to the architecture program. Trevor was in his second year in the program and was already lobbying for Terrence to think about it as a career. But Terrence couldn't decide yet between environmental science and architecture. Maybe he would be like Chase and major in more than one thing.

They explored theatres, art buildings, and departments covering everything from law to dentistry. They even got to tour some dorm rooms. Terrence's mother noted that Trevor didn't let them see his room, which meant he must have laundry all over the floor. Trevor did not object.

Of course, the highlight of the visit was eating in the cafeteria.

"I'll tell you, the food in Washington, DC does not disappoint. If this is how they feed you in college, sign me up now!" said Chase between bites.

"You can't pick a college just because they have good food," Akiya objected.

"Prove it," said Marcus, licking his fingers and pushing his empty tray away.

"Have you boys listened to anything on this tour besides your stomachs?" asked Ebony sarcastically.

"Yes. I was already sold on the academics. Now I'm sold on the food." Chase laughed.

Trevor let the group know it was time for them to view some of the recreational facilities and to see how college students spent their time when they weren't in class.

Rebekah raised her hand.

"No need to raise your hand, feel free to ask away," he told her.

"I know this is called a historically Black college. Does that mean you have to be Black to come?"

"That is a great question!" said Trevor, and he really did seem excited. "The answer is no, absolutely not. We have plenty of non-Black students here at Howard, but in any given year, there can be a higher percentage of Black students here at Howard, or, really, most other historically black colleges, than the percentage of African Americans you may find at predominantly White institutions. So, if you like what you see, if anyone likes what they see, I hope you put Howard on your list of potential schools you might want to consider when it is time for you to go to college, if that is in your plans."

"I definitely will!" said Rebekah.

***

The group continued on with the tour, and there seemed to be no end to the number of interesting spaces to explore. When their legs were tired and their stomachs started to growl again, Trevor let the group know it was time to head out to the bus.

As they were about to board the bus, Trevor called out to Terrence. "And where are the STEAM Chasers going? I'm not done with you all."

"What?" Terrence was surprised by this.

"I told you I had some things planned. Now, can I see Shar, Ebony, and Akiya?"

The three stepped up to see Trevor. Most of the other students had gotten on the bus and were looking out the windows at what was happening. Three girls who looked like they were college students came up beside Trevor.

"Are these our new friends?" asked one.

"Absolutely!" he said, smiling.

"Well, we heard that you three were pretty excited about maybe joining a sorority one day. In the meantime, we have a little gift for you right now."

Each girl pulled out a sweatshirt. One was pink and green and had the Greek letters AKA across the front. Another sweatshirt was red and white and had the words Delta Sigma Theta in bold letters. The final sweatshirt was blue and white with the Greek letters for Zeta Phi Beta.

"One for each of you. This means you are each an official little sister!" said one of the girls.

Shar, Ebony, and Akiya hugged each of the girls and put on their new sweaters.

"Have you all ever heard of the saying the Divine Nine?" asked Trevor.

They nodded their heads.

"Well," he began, "the National Pan-Hellenic Council makes up the African American Greek-lettered fraternities and sororities. There are nine altogether and so they are often referred to as the Divine Nine. The NPHC was started right here on Howard's campus back in nineteen thirty. So, as a treat to the class, we are letting every single one of you leave with a reminder that when you are ready for us, we'll be right here ready for you."

Six more students joined the three that had given the sweaters to Ebony, Akiya, and Shar. They had their arms filled with tee shirts and hats. They had Greek letters or words saying Kappa Alpha Psi, Omega Psi Phi, Alpha Kappa Alpha, Delta Sigma Theta, Zeta Phi Beta, Alpha Phi Alpha, Phi Beta Sigma, Sigma Gamma Rho, and Iota Phi Theta, indicating they were little brothers, little sisters, or future members. Every single class member got a gift from at least one of the Divine Nine organizations. Once again, Trevor had pulled through with something big.

Once everyone was settled back onto the bus, Terrence looked over to see Shar, Ebony, and Akiya still talking and smiling wildly. Maybe the boys would be forgiven for their prank after all!

 Chapter 16

The next day, it was time to pack and prepare for the airport. Terrence couldn't believe it was already time to go. It seemed like there was so much left to learn.

As they all headed downstairs with their luggage, it appeared as if everyone was thinking the same thing. People seemed to be moving slowly on purpose.

Mrs. Worthington must have picked up on this.

"I understand we all wish we could stay a bit longer. But we packed a lot into this trip. And I know you all got enough information to complete some projects to share with your classmates and maybe even the rest of the school."

This seemed to re-energize the group. Everyone loved Mrs. Worthington's projects. She let groups have complete control over what their final projects looked like as long as the team included a short paper to go along with it.

***

Once they got to the airport, Mrs. Worthington passed out the plane tickets.

"Whelp, see you all once we land back home," said Chase.

"Look at your ticket first." Mrs. Faulkner, who was helping Mrs. Worthington get students checked in, laughed.

Chase opened his ticket. "I'm in seat eight A."

Marcus opened his next. "I'm in seat eight B!"

Terrence held his breath and opened his ticket. "Seat eight C!"

"We confessed to Principal Davis as soon as we landed," said Shar. "And he said you boys deserved it."

"Plus, he didn't seem too bad to sit with. He had some great information," added Akiya.

"Well, what seats are you all in?" asked Terrence.

Shar was in seat 9A, Ebony in 9B, and Akiya in 9C.

"That is perfect! We have a lot of work to do," said Terrence.

"Work, what work?" asked Marcus.

"We need to start planning our strategy. We need to figure out the Blackprint, remember?" said Terrence.

"Of course, the Blackprint is going to be fabulous!" said Marcus.

As they all got settled into their seats on the plane, Chase looked at the group and said, "I wonder what is the Blackprint in our hometown?"

"You know, I never thought of that." Terrence sat back, wondering why he never had this thought.

"I wonder if any of our parents are a part of the Blackprint," said Akiya. "I mean we learned about twin sisters and companies over a hundred years old."

"Plus, we found out the Blackprint even goes all the way to places like Tokyo, Japan and Paris, France," said Ebony.

Shar sat back and smiled. "The Blackprint is pretty boundless."

Ebony looked at Shar. "You know, that's true. Look at all the things we learned when we were at Space Camp!"

"Well, now that we know the Blackprint exists and it is pretty much everyone, we need to figure out how to help other people find and recognize the Blackprint where they are," said Chase.

"Plus, we have a crime to correct, right?" Terrence reached out his hand to give a fist bump to Chase.

"So, Detective, how should we get this mystery solved? We owe it to **Marie Van Brittan Brown** and **Bessie Blount Griffin**!" said Chase.

***

The STEAM Chasers met before and after school every day for a week to try to figure out how to bring the Blackprint to reality.

There were a lot of ideas passed back and forth between the group. Chase said they could make an app that would allow a person to scan any space they were in and see if it was a part of the Blackprint. If so, the person would get to learn about the history of the individual who created it.

Marcus wanted to commission drone pilots from all over the country to film every Blackprint space and donate all the footage to the National Museum of African American History and Culture.

Akiya thought it would be a good idea to create an encyclopedia of the Blackprint where there could be print and digital copies that would be updated annually.

"We should have known, Akiya and books," laughed Marcus. Akiya smiled and shook her head at Marcus.

Ebony suggested they create a computer game people could play to learn about the Blackprint. Of course, people who made a high score would see rockets blasting off, culminating in a fireworks show similar to the one they helped create.

Shar had a great idea of creating a special award that people could win for correcting the Blackprint and making sure individuals got the credit they deserved. Of course, Chase thought this would be a great idea since he thought he would receive the first prize.

Terrence came up with the solution the group loved, they would do all of those things. He took Chase and Ebony's ideas and figured they could work together developing an app that would include fun and interactive games people could play as they filled in the Blackprint missing from their own communities. Terrence figured that kids all over the country could go through their communities and find where the Blackprint was, then report it back to be entered into Akiya's idea of a book, sort of like an encyclopedia. People who found Blackprint corrections could win awards, and he wouldn't even mind giving Chase the first one. And, an army of drones could go out and put special tags on all those spaces so that as people walked through their communities, it would be easy for them to spot the Blackprint right there in front of them.

"Okay, that's our big idea, but where do we start?" Asked Ebony, looking at Terrence in anticipation.

"Right here, right now." He grabbed a notebook out of his backpack. "Let's go hunting for the Blackprint in our town."

"Right there with you," said Chase. "There is just one thing I need to do." Chase was finishing up an email. "Ten down, and a lot more to go."

"What do you mean?" Asked Akiya?

"I'm sending an email to all the sites that have the wrong picture for **Marie Van Brittan Brown**. We have to start somewhere, right?"

And with that, the STEAM Chasers were ready to take on their biggest assignment yet. They hoped lots of other kids would join them for the journey.